America Falls

Episode 4

Rude Shock

SCOTT MEDBURY

ISBN: 9781981032815

DEDICATION

For my wife Joanne, you're my everything.

CONTENTS

ACKNOWLEDGMENTS

To everyone who has encouraged, supported and badgered me (in a nice way) to finish the trilogy, thank you..

"Inside every man is a beast that cannot be tamed…" –Anonymous

Rude Shock

SCOTT MEDBURY

Part One -The Valley

SCOTT MEDBURY

1

The optimism we felt that day, looking down at the farmhouse, was overwhelming and infectious. We rushed down the hill to what would become our new home like crazy, excited kids and, right then, that's exactly what we were. All of the death and destruction was forgotten for a little while and we were able to just be ourselves.

The big farmhouse dominated the fields and buildings around it. It looked sturdy and well maintained despite its faded paintwork and, like the others, I felt a burst of happiness at the prospect we would make it our home.

Ben was the first to reach the verandah which wrapped around the entire building, only slowing as he climbed the stairs and arrived at the front door. It was painted a jarring shade of pale blue and looked as if it could have been painted just yesterday. Ben waited for the rest of us to arrive, wanting to share the moment, I guess. We gathered round and we seemed to collectively hold our breath as he reached out and grasped the brass door handle before turning it. It was locked.

"Of course," said Ben. "Wouldn't want things to be too easy now, would we?"

I stepped forward and put my ear to the door. I couldn't hear anything. Indigo had gone to a window and peeked past the white lace curtains.

"Nothing."

"I think it's safe to break in," I said. "But let's try not to damage the door too much."

"I'll do it," volunteered Ben. He stepped back a few paces, ushering the rest of us out of the way, then shoulder charged the door ... and promptly fell on his backside, leaving the door unscathed and us in stitches.

"I'll try," said Beau from the rear of our group, as Ben climbed to his feet, rubbing his shoulder and looking sheepish.

We let him through and he produced a small red-handled chisel from his pocket.

"Where did you get that?" asked Luke.

"Back at one of the houses we raided. It was in the garage."

He stepped up to the door and placed the point of the chisel where the door met the jamb, just next to the handle, and began working it. It wasn't an easy task, but after a few minutes and several of us having turns, there was a splintering sound as the latch pulled free of the timber and the door creaked open.

"Ben and I will go in first and scope it out," I said, pulling out my handgun. "I'll yell the all clear when we're sure it's okay."

The house was big, empty, and well maintained. The room we entered was a big living room with a high ceiling and a large brick fireplace. It was furnished comfortably, if not extravagantly, the older style furniture reminding me of houses I had seen in old black and white movies my mom and dad used to watch occasionally.

Opposite the front door was a staircase leading up to a landing that ran the equivalent length of the living room. We decided to explore the ground level first.

To the left was a large kitchen and with a huge walk-in pantry and a door that led down to a large basement. We high fived when we saw how well-stocked it was. A door at the rear of the kitchen led to a laundry. We also found a bathroom on ground floor and then headed for the stairs.

On the landing, we decided to split up to explore the upper level of the big house. We were almost certainly the only humans in there, dead or alive. While the home smelt musty, there was no nasty undertone of rot to it and I'm pretty sure if anyone was living there we would have been confronted by now.

We found six bedrooms on the upper level, along with another bathroom and, as I suspected, there were no bodies, dead or alive, in any of the rooms. We reached the last bedroom together; it appeared to be the master bedroom and had a massive four poster bed.

We looked around. I checked the wardrobe as Ben examined the big timber dresser against the back wall. He picked up a tiny crystal object from where it sat on the polished top.

"I think I'll give this to Brooke," he said. "She always loved Bambi when we were little."

I felt a pang of loss as I thought briefly of my own sister.

"I think she'd like that. I better call them up. They must be wondering what's happening."

I went to the door.

"All clear! Come on in!"

The squeals of sheer delight and thundering footsteps on the staircase were infectious and Ben and I looked at each other, grinning. Apparently, we had the same idea and immediately ran for the big bed, leaping onto it and rolling onto our backs. It probably wasn't the smartest thing to do while packing loaded guns, but we were oblivious.

We lay there spread-eagle on the soft mattress, laughing and listening to doors slam and voices call dibs on rooms and I felt myself begin to slowly relax. It had been a long, difficult journey, but I felt like, at last, we were finally home.

A grinning Luke joined us shortly thereafter and instigated a pillow fight by grabbing one from the floor where it had fallen and whacking me one handed in the side of the head. Outnumbered four good arms to one, he lost badly!

It appeared the house had been vacant at the

time of the infection and, while Ben, Luke, and I were acting out upstairs along with the others, Indigo and Brooke, far more practical than us, were checking the pantry. Ben and I had looked briefly, of course, but the girls went through it and made an inventory of everything in there. It was extremely well-stocked, with an assortment of canned foods and dry packaged goods, like flour and sugar. It appeared we had really struck the motherlode.

We spent the next few hours exploring every nook and cranny of our new home. The house had its own generator, which Beau managed to fire up. We would be able to power the house, at least until we ran out of fuel for the generator. There were a few modern appliances, including a stove and oven in the kitchen and a TV in the living room, but apart from that, it was pretty much technology-free. The big fireplace in the living room would definitely come in handy once winter set in.

As the girls prepared a warm meal -- our first since we had escaped from Drake Mountain -- I couldn't resist turning on the TV. I flicked through the stations slowly, knowing I wouldn't find anything, except possibly Chinese broadcasts, but hoping just the same. Apart from one channel which had a black screen, all the rest were digital snow.

"Nothing, huh?" Luke asked, coming up beside me.

"Nah. Didn't think there would be, but ... you know."

"I thought there would be a Chinese channel, at least. It might be a sign the Professor's attack was successful."

"Maybe. I guess we'll find out soon enough."

During our trek from Drake Mountain, I had reconciled my mixed emotions regarding the retaliatory attack on the Chinese. As we passed the empty houses and towns which were a testament to the ruthlessness of the Chinese government, I wondered how we could ever remain free while a regime like that established itself in our country.

While it was horrible that thousands would die if the reverse engineered virus had been effective, there was no other way we were ever going to have a chance to live out our lives as free people if it wasn't. Perhaps the end did justify the means after all.

"Yeah ... hey, on a brighter note, there are a few animals out in the yard, but I don't think it was a functioning farm. Not for a long time anyway. I think it was more like a hobby farm. Probably owned by some rich city dude who only came on the weekends or something."

"Yeah, or maybe it was a bed and breakfast," said Brooke, coming up beside us and looking at the black screen. "What's on? Oh, I think I've seen this show. It's called Blackout, right?"

We laughed at her lame joke and Luke grabbed her in a bear hug. The pretty English girl squealed in delight as she struggled to escape his grip. He let her go eventually and she told us that dinner was ready as she left the room looking happy.

"What?" asked Luke, when he saw my knowing smile.

"Huh? Oh, nothing... nothing at all. Just thinking you two would make a great couple."

He blushed and I slapped him on his good shoulder.

"Come on, let's go eat."

The meal Brooke and Indigo had prepared was nothing fancy, but it was a feast to us. Although it was dinnertime, the mix of foods on the table would actually have made a hearty breakfast.

Beau had collected eggs from an abandoned chicken coop he found. It appeared the chickens were now free range, but apparently came back to the coop to lay. Indigo had fried them up so they were crisp on the bottom and soft on top. We had one each with a couple left over. Luke and Ben wolfed those down when everyone else politely passed. No one seemed to mind.

The fried eggs were delicious and to accompany them we had oatmeal, warm baked beans, and, for dessert, a crusty kind of homemade bread with honey on top.

"I propose a toast," said Luke, banging his fork against the glass of water in front of him. "Here's to fresh eggs!"

We all laughed and spent the next hour happily enjoying food, friendship, and the comfort of our new home.

After dinner, Indigo, Brooke, and I chipped in to clear the table and wash the dishes, while the others went upstairs. There was something strangely comforting about that domestic chore, and I found myself enjoying it and the company of the girls almost as much as I had enjoyed dinner. It was something none of us had done for a very long time. For me, it was topped off when Brooke left the room briefly and Indigo grasped my face with hands covered in soap suds and kissed me on the lips as I dried a bowl. Of course, the tender moment was cut short by Luke entering at that most inopportune moment.

"Get a room, you two!"

His teasing earned him a swift punch in the arm from Brooke who trailed behind him. I was too happy at the sweet promise that kiss held to let anything faze me. Indigo and I just giggled and went back to washing the dishes.

When we had finished, Allie made everyone a drink of hot chocolate from cocoa powder and Carnation evaporated milk. We drank it standing up in the kitchen as the conversation turned more serious.

"We need to vote for a leader," said Paul, after draining his mug in record time. "I nominate Isaac. He's done a good job so far and I don't see a reason we should change."

"Do we really need a leader?" asked Allie. "I mean, we all get along and stuff."

"Yeah, we do," said Brooke. "A strong one. I

for one don't want to see a pig's head on a stake any time. If we were on an island, I would be freaking out right now."

I understood her reference to William Golding's Lord of the Flies, but there were some blank looks on faces around the room. Luke briefly explained, with some relish, the characters' descent into savagery and murder, evoking expressions of horror from Ava and Allie.

"Well, thanks for that cheerful explanation, Luke," said Ben. "The point is, we do need a leader. I vote for Isaac, too. Anyone else?"

Hands went up around the room and I found myself unanimously elected for a position I hadn't volunteered for, elected as leader without opening my mouth. Indigo squeezed my arm supportively. I was quiet for a moment. Thing was, I wasn't sure I wanted to shoulder all the responsibility again.

"I'm really flattered. But truth is, I couldn't have been a good leader without everyone else doing their part, too. I don't want to lead on my own.... I nominate Indigo and Luke to be my co-leaders."

"Do you mean like advisors or actual co-leaders?" asked Luke.

"Co-leaders. I want each of us to have an equal say."

"A triumvirate then? Yeah, I'm cool with that."

"A what?" asked Ava.

"It's a Roman term," said Luke. "During one period of their history, instead of being ruled by one man, they were ruled by three who all had equal power."

"Well," I said quickly. "We're not ruling anyone; we'll be leading, which is different. And with three of us making the decisions, there is less chance of someone doing something stupid. What do you say, Indigo?"

She looked unsure, but when all the girls piped up in support, she smiled and agreed.

"Okay, I guess." She shrugged. "If that's what everybody wants. I think we should vote again in six months or something to give someone else a chance though."

"Maybe a year?" suggested Luke. "Shall we take a vote then? All those in favor of Isaac, Indigo, and myself being our first triumvirate, raise your hand."

Everybody's hands went up.

"And voting every year?"

Again the vote was unanimous. I guess that vote was the first step we took to planning our future. The very fact that we'd been in the Valley for just a few hours and were already scheduling something in a year's time displayed the sense of optimism we all felt.

Over the next forty or so minutes, we managed to assign jobs and tasks for everyone and also decided it would be wise for the time being to set a nightly watch, just in case there were other not-so-friendly inhabitants in the area. Beau volunteered for that night's first shift and it was agreed he would wake Paul at 3 A.M. to take over until morning.

It was Indigo who brought up the sleeping arrangements.

"So, what shall we do about the bedrooms?"

"Um, girls sharing with girls and boys sharing with boys," I said, too fast.

I could feel my face burning. I had decided earlier I would suggest that arrangement, so why was I embarrassed? Probably because of Luke's wicked grin and my own teenage awkwardness.

Of course, as soon as the words were out of my mouth, I started to think that maybe Indigo would think I didn't want to share a room with her. I mean, I had just assumed she wouldn't want to share with me, but I definitely didn't want her to think that I didn't want to share with her ... just in case she did want to! I was very confused.

She came to my rescue.

"Okay," she said, a little smile curling her lips. "Sounds good. Brooke and I can have the room with the single beds and Ava and Allie can bunk together in the big room."

"Are you sure?" asked Ava. "I can have a single bed if you want."

"No, don't be silly" said Brooke. "In your condition, I think you deserve the big bed."

"Okay cool," I said, the roaring flames of my embarrassment slowly dying to embers. "I'll share with Luke."

"I'll share with Beau," said Paul.

"Excellent! I'll have a room all too myself!" said

Ben.

After that awkward conversation, I brought up a far more serious one.

"It's been a few days now since the Professor's drones went out. I want to take a small group scouting to see what's happened. I plan to head back to Plymouth on foot to survey the damage ... if there is any. It shouldn't take more than a day and night. We'll leave before dawn the day after tomorrow. Any volunteers?"

Ava was the only one who didn't put her hand up. Given her condition, I wasn't surprised.

"Not you, Luke, you only lost your hand a few days ago. I want you to rest up and let it heal properly."

For once he didn't argue.

"Ben and Paul, I'll take you two. Indigo and Brooke, I'd rather you two stay and help Allie make sure everything runs smoothly the first few days. Beau, I want you to start getting the farm and the animals we have into shape. Luke can help as much as he can. Ava, you just need to rest up and look after you and the baby."

I told them I would organize the mission the next day and we began discussing our plans for the farm and writing the list of chores for everyone to do. Among us, only Beau had any kind of farm experience. During our journey to the Valley, he had told us he had spent many a summer holiday on his uncle's farm in Vermont.

We had an ample water supply. The pond at the rear of the property was huge and there was also a large rainwater tank adjacent to the farmhouse. Luke informed us the tank water would be okay to drink but we should still to go through the process of boiling our drinking water. Of course, we would have to do the same with the pond water if we ever needed it. We set up a roster for someone to collect water from the tank and boil it every day.

Like the chicken coop, we had found the gates to the pig pen open when we arrived and one of the girls had since spotted the escapees roaming the farm. With a bit of luck, they would all be on the farm somewhere. Beau's first task would be to catch the pigs and the chickens with the help of a few volunteers.

The cattle were in good shape, grass being in plentiful supply. There were four cows, a calf, and a bull, but only the mother was giving milk. Another was pregnant and Beau informed us she would be ready to milk after she gave birth.

"The other two are kind of useless for milk unless they become pregnant. Two should produce plenty of milk for us, though."

"That bull's been a busy boy," opined Ben. "Maybe he's taking turns."

"Yeah ... well, we'll have to get him into another paddock so we can work with the cows. We'll take care of the pigs first, though."

Much to Luke's amusement, Paul, who had

actually put us on the path to the farm, was horrified at the thought of milking a cow when it was suggested we make a roster for that chore, too.

"Dude, it's easy," said Luke, demonstrating. His arms moved up and down, his good hand squeezed air while his bandaged stump moved up and down in sync. "You just grip and squeeze ... grip and squeeze."

We all laughed. All except Brook. I noticed a tear glinting on her cheek in the candlelight. Luke noticed, too. His smile turned rueful and he brought his stump up and looked at it.

"Yeah, I miss it, too. It's like my hand is still there sometimes. It aches and I swear I can even feel my fingers, but when I check ... well, it's just old stumpy here. Which reminds me, I think bionic hands are in short supply these days, so I will need a hook. That's my first order of business."

"No badass post-apocalyptic survivor should be without one," said Ben, trying to lighten the mood. "I was pretty handy at metalworking at school, so when we get back I'll help, if you need it."

"Thanks, that'd be cool."

As we were saying our goodnights, Ben took the opportunity to give Brooke the crystal reindeer.

"Oh! Thank you, Ben, it's beautiful."

She kissed her brother on the cheek looking happier than she had a few minutes before.

It had been another long walk to reach the farm and now the excitement had worn off and we were all tired. Still a little awkward from the discussion about sleeping arrangements, I hung back awkwardly as everyone got up and went their separate ways. Indigo wasn't awkward though, she made her way between bodies and grasped my hand in hers before whispering in my ear.

"You're so cute."

I blushed again, secretly pleased at her compliment as she pulled me towards the hall doorway. We made our way up the stairs hand in hand and, at the top, she kissed me gently on the lips. "Get a good night's sleep. I'll see you in the morning."

"Okay," I said, a sense of well-being washing over me. This new stage of our adventure had started off better than I could have imagined.

2

The next day was busy, but a lot of fun. In the morning, we all pitched in to catch the pigs and chickens. It took at least three hours and, by the time we were done, all of us were dirty, tired, and, in some cases, bleeding from our efforts.

We congratulated ourselves as we ate a lunch of Spam and mustard on Indigo's homemade bread. The sandwiches were tasty but a little hard to swallow without a swig of water.

"Sorry, they're so dry," said Indigo, as she washed down a mouthful. "We have no butter."

"I'll make some this afternoon," Beau promised.

Our morning tally of recaptured animals came to three pigs and seven hens. We were pretty confident we had all the pigs, but there had been sightings of more rogue chickens.

"Now the hard part, time to get the bull out of the cow paddock," said Beau, as he licked a final few crumbs from his fingers.

"This should be fun," said Luke. "I'll meet you

there."

He jumped up and ran towards the farmhouse.

"Where is he going?" Beau asked.

"Best not to ask," Brooke laughed. "He'll probably come back dressed as a bullfighter."

We all laughed, but in the end she wasn't far wrong. Luke joined us at the gate to the main paddock carrying a small, bright red towel as we eyed the massive beast nervously. At his arrival, the bull swung his heavy, impossibly large head around and looked directly at us. The three cows and the calf didn't pay us any mind as they chewed grass happily.

"Dude! Put that thing behind your back, will you?"

I know it was impossible, but the look in his baleful, black eyes told me the bull knew exactly what we were up to.

"Whoa!" said Luke. "He looks even bigger today."

He carefully slipped his good hand behind his back, tucking the towel into the waist of his jeans.

"I thought it was a myth about them not liking red," Indigo said out of the corner of her mouth. Her eyes were glued to the beast.

"It is," Luke said shrugging. "But you gotta keep traditions, right? Okay, who is doing this with me?"

He walked purposefully to the gate and grabbed the handle, ready to pull back the bolt. I stood up and so did Ben.

"Right, what's the plan?" asked the English boy.

Beau pointed to the far end of the big paddock.

"There is the gate you need to get him through. Once he's through you can close it and he'll be stuck in the smaller paddock all on his own. I'll go around and unlatch it. I'll swing it open when you get him there."

Thankfully, the bull seemed to have forgotten about us and had gone back to his grazing.

"Okay," said Luke, sounding much braver than I felt.

He pulled open the gate and we three walked slowly in. Luke closed the gate and reached over and shot the bolt home. Beau was already running quietly along the other side of the fence to the other paddock.

"Okay, let's walk part of the way to the other gate. For the moment, stay close to the fence," Luke whispered.

We must have looked comical as we began to tiptoe through the long grass not taking our eyes off the bull.

"Be careful," Allie called from behind us and the bull's head shot up.

Now, we've all heard the saying scared the shit out of me. I don't know if that's actually possible, but right in that moment I think I came the closest I've ever come to doing just that. My guts felt like they'd turned to water and my heart hurt with the shot of adrenalin that jolted me.

"Don't move," Luke whispered, as we all froze in place.

A few seconds went by as I willed the bull to go back to his grazing. He didn't. He took one heavy step, then another towards us, and paused and snorted. I felt relief. It was short lived. The bull stamped the ground twice and then charged. He reminded me of a steam train my dad had taken us to see once. He started off slow, seeming to struggle with his own weight, but soon he was steaming along invisible tracks towards us.

"Run!" Luke shrieked, unnecessarily.

I was already in motion. Beside me, Luke pulled the red flag out of his jeans and began to wave it around screaming at the top of his lungs.

"Come and get me, you big, ugly bastard!"

I didn't even look over my shoulder, I was too focused on getting the hell out of there. It wasn't until I heard screams of terror behind us that I looked back. Ben wasn't with us. In fact, he hadn't moved. He was frozen in fear against the fence, his mouth agape as the bull barreled towards him. We stopped and looked helplessly at our friend.

"Ben! Run, you idiot!" I yelled.

It was too late. If he ran now, the bull would mow him down like a steam train rolling over a rabbit.

"Fuck ..." Luke moaned.

I scrunched up my face in anticipation of the

impact. Miraculously, at the last possible moment, Ben seemed to come to his senses and, squealing like a girl, moved quicker than I had ever seen him move before. He turned and almost without touching it, scaled the gate, falling on his face behind it as the bull collided into it.

Not only the gate but the whole fence shook and trembled with the terrific impact. For a second, I thought it might fall, but it held. The bull reeled back, almost falling to its haunches before shaking its stunned head in a very human way as it steadied itself on four wobbly legs.

I sighed in relief at Ben's escape, but barely had time to draw a breath before Luke again called out.

"Run!"

The bull was already charging again and I turned on my heels and ran for my life ... literally. Luke was waving the red towel and yelling obscenities at the bull. If I'd been able to, I would have told him to shut up, but I didn't have breath to spare.

I could see Beau at the gate about thirty yards ahead. He had already pulled it open and was yelling with a look of horror on his face, beckoning wildly for us to hurry. Luke had stopped yelling and waving the stupid towel and was concentrating on pumping his arms in order to get as much velocity as he could. His look of horror mirrored how I imagined my own looked... and if the situation hadn't been so potentially deadly, I probably would have laughed.

It felt like we had run a mile as we closed on

the opening and I would have felt relief, but the thundering of hooves directly behind me told me I was in imminent danger. I heard faint screams behind me and in front Beau sprinted out of the opening to the side ready to slide the gate back home when the bull was through.

The thud of the hooves closed on me and I could now hear a rhythmic snorting, like the bellows of a steam train. I envisioned two sharp horns closing in on my butt and pushed my chest out like a runner about to break the ribbon of a finishing line.

If it had been a race, Luke and I would have tied. We crossed the threshold to the other yard in a dead heat and I veered right as he veered left, the direction Beau had gone. I heard Luke whoop and I was about to do the same when something hard connected with my hip and sent me flying. Luke swore later that I flew at least ten feet. My legs were still pumping as I landed and was carried face first into the grass by my own momentum. Behind me, I heard a mewling kind of roar and a heavy thump and skid.

On hands and knees, my chest heaving, I glanced in the bull's direction. When I had veered right after passing through the gate, the bull had swung its head and struck me a glancing blow but in the process had knocked itself off balance and skidded into the turf. Now it was struggling back into a standing position.

My hip throbbed, but apart from that I was

relatively unscathed. I wasn't about to stretch the friendship any further and quickly rose on wobbly legs and ran back towards the gate.

"Hurry up, dude! He's coming!" called Luke.

Once again I heard the horrible, thumping pursuit of hooves and found an extra burst of energy. I passed through the gate and the boys slammed it home. The bull pulled up clumsily, just short of crashing into the gate, apparently having learnt a lesson after his earlier collision.

A wave of relief washed over me and I fell to the grass and rolled onto my back, peering at the sky as I got my breath back.

Luke and Beau soon fell to the grass behind me. Luke was the first to giggle.

"Dude, the look on your face ..." his giggle turned to a laugh and soon Beau and I joined in, slowly at first, then more heartily. Pretty soon we were all holding our stomachs and squirming on the grass in helpless amusement.

Our friends, who had been watching on helplessly, were less amused and Luke and I both received a scolding.

3

After our close encounter of the bovine kind we headed back to the farmhouse, where Ben, Paul, and I sat down and put together a plan for the mission into Plymouth.

We would leave at dawn the following morning, each of us armed with handguns and also carrying a few spare clips of ammunition in our backpacks. If the virus had been effective and had done what it was designed to do, we expected to return with more weapons and ammo and whatever supplies we could bring with us. Our success would all depend on what had happened over the past few days. If the Chinese were unaffected, it was unlikely we would be able to bring anything back, but at least we would have the intel.

The three of us had an early night that evening, going to bed just after dinner and sleeping in the same room so as not to disturb the others when we were woken by Indigo, who had volunteered to wake us just before dawn. I took this as a sign she couldn't bear for me to leave without saying goodbye and I fell asleep thinking of her.

I was tired and felt like I had barely been asleep

a few minutes when Indigo's gentle shaking woke me.

"Time to get up, sleepyhead," she whispered, and kissed my forehead.

Remarkable what a little kiss can do. I suddenly didn't feel so tired anymore and jumped out of bed, regretting it instantly as my bruised hip protested loudly. I swallowed the discomfort and helped her wake the other two before grabbing my coat and boots and following her downstairs.

We each ate a can of SpaghettiOs and a slice of Indigo's homemade bread for breakfast. Not as nutritious as it could have been, but I had turned down her offer to fry us some eggs. I wanted to get going as soon as we could.

"I cannot wait for that cooked chicken you promised when we get back, Indigo," said Paul, looking distastefully into the bottom of the SpaghettiOs can. Despite the look, he was doing a fantastic job of getting every last drop of sauce out of it.

"Yep, I'll get to work on it while you're gone. Tomorrow night, hopefully," she said.

I wolfed my SpaghettiOs down. The two cooked meals we had enjoyed since arriving hadn't yet killed off my instinct to eat as much as I could when I could. I grabbed a small backpack and began to stock it with the cans of food Indigo had gathered for us. We also had enough water to get us through the next twenty-four hours.

"If it's safe, I'm hoping we can bring more food

back with us, too."

"Amen," said Ben. "And I want some boots. These shitty canvas shoes are just about done."

"Good thinking. We'll try to bring back clothing, as well."

"Are you thinking we'll be able to steal a vehicle?" asked Paul.

"Yeah," I said, after a moment. "Hopefully, we won't even have to steal one. If the Professor's virus was as lethal as it was on Sonny, I have a feeling we will have Plymouth pretty much to ourselves."

"If it is safe and you see a drugstore, we need some 'girl' items too," said Indigo.

This time I wasn't the only one who went red. Indigo sighed in mock exasperation.

"Don't worry boys, I'll write you a list."

We were ready to leave a half-hour later. By then, Luke had awoken too and he and Indigo walked us out onto the creaky verandah just as the sun was just starting to lighten the sky in the east. Ben and Paul stepped off the verandah and began talking quietly as I turned to Indigo.

We kissed briefly and then embraced.

"Be careful, Isaac."

"I will ... you too. Don't let anyone get complacent. We don't know how safe this place is yet."

We kissed again and I gave her a wave and stepped down to join Paul and Ben and shake Luke's hand.

"Be careful out there," said Luke, a serious look on his face. "Any threat, use extreme prejudice. Don't think ... act."

"Thanks, Rambo," I said, smiling.

"I'm serious, dude."

"I know," I said, putting my hand up. "Don't worry, we'll be careful."

We said our goodbyes and, with a last look over my shoulder at Indigo, we began to walk up the sloping driveway towards the gate.

4

It was slow going until the sun came up. The morning was cold and I felt for Paul and Ben. While I still had the boots from my brief stint as a soldier back at Drake Mountain, they still wore the canvas shoes they had been supplied when we had arrived. The flimsy shoes were really inadequate for anything but indoor use, and after our long walk from the facility to the Valley, they were pretty much worn out. To their credit, they didn't complain, apart from the occasional obscenity when stepping on a sharp stone.

Even with their footwear issues, we made good time as a group of three and reached the southern tip of Squam Lake in just a few hours. We rested there a while and ate some Hershey's Bars Indigo had found in the farmhouse pantry.

The day had warmed considerably by then and Ben suggested we go 'bathing' before we headed off again. Paul looked at the English boy as if he had lost his mind. I started laughing.

"He means go for a swim."

"Oh," said Paul, and raised his arm, sniffing under it.

I didn't think I smelled that bad. "It sounds

great, but shouldn't we keep going? Besides we don't have towels and I don't want to walk while I am wet."

"Yeah, we don't really have time, Ben. I want to get this over and done with."

Ben shrugged.

"Okay, you go on ahead. I'll be with you in a second."

Without waiting for a response, he jogged over to the water and gracefully dived, fully clothed, into the water. He surfaced a few seconds later then swam out about thirty feet before swimming back to shore and emerging soaking wet.

"I don't know if that was such a good idea," Paul said, laughing, the squeaking, slushing sound of Ben's wet shoes punctuating each step he took. "If the Chinese aren't dead or gone, they'll hear you coming a mile off."

By the time we reached Route 175, I was regretting I hadn't followed Ben's lead. While the morning had been cool, the late winter's day was unseasonably warm and the forest that lined the blacktop seemed to contain the heat. It would be a warm summer.

We stayed on the road this time. It was faster and easier to walk. In the event of a Chinese vehicle coming from either direction, I was confident we would be able to hear it and get into the trees before we were spotted. A couple of hours after Ben's impromptu swim we took a left onto 175A which led right into Plymouth. At that point, when we could, we travelled closer to the tree line and hurried past those spots where the trees were further back from the road.

After about four hours, we reached an underpass bordering the eastern fringe of Plymouth and stopped to drink, eat, and rest before we went into town. Not only was it cool in the shade of the underpass, it gave us good cover from which we could survey the road ahead.

We hadn't heard the sound of choppers or any other aircraft since leaving the Valley and, even as we approached Plymouth, we didn't see or hear any vehicles. From the shadows of the underpass, I could see a gas station about two hundred yards down on the left. It had some vehicles in front but we could see no movement. Further on, there was no traffic on the road or any other sign of life, for that matter.

"We didn't come this close on our way past last time and we saw plenty of vehicles," said Paul, in a low voice.

"Yes, you're right," Ben said. "It's definitely not as busy as it was on our way past."

Naively, I had half-expected we would see bodies lying on the road if the attack had been successful, but, of course, the nature of the virus meant any casualties would not have been instantly incapacitated. Like our own victims of the virus, most would have been bedridden or indoors hours or days before dying.

I didn't speak for a minute. We were only on the outskirts of town, so I wasn't absolutely convinced the attack had been successful. I wouldn't relax until I saw evidence for myself. We would still need to be cautious going forward. I pulled my weapon out of my pocket and indicated they should do the same.

"Stay alert. We won't know for sure until we get right into town. Until then, we need to be extra careful."

The main road into Plymouth offered little in the way of cover so we moved to the left and, with our weapons in hand, jogged across the mouth of a road to a copse of trees bordering the gas station we had seen from the underpass.

Sticking to the shadows, we slunk to the edge of the driveway. The gas station was deserted, but it didn't appear to be that long since it had been in use. The gardens were neat and the white painted building was tidy and well maintained. The only element of discord was the large Chinese flag atop the flagpole. The blazing red of the ensign jarred the senses when viewed in such a typically small town America setting.

"Looks like they made themselves right at home," said Paul, bitterly.

I scanned the area and spotted a camouflaged Humvee at the end of the long drive that went down the left side of the building and into the back of the lot. I slotted that information away in my memory bank. If everything went well, we might be able to load it up and drive it back to the Valley. I pointed it out to the others.

"We'll come back for that. Let's get moving."

The abandoned gas station was promising, but at this point I still wasn't willing to take risks until we saw more.

We moved on cautiously, passing a Citgo gas station further down the road to the left and an overgrown baseball field to the right. Again, there were a few cars parked in the Citgo, but no signs of life.

We passed something that looked like a rental car business, its lot full of white cars in need of a wash. If worse came to worse, we could raid it and take one or two of those cars, but I would prefer a Hummer ...or two.

We stopped and squatted in the shade of a large, neat, red brick building. I quickly surveyed the road ahead before turning my attention back to the building. The wall above us was marred by a large, white Chinese character. It was spray painted on and I was curious to know what it meant. The building looked like it may have been a library in its previous incarnation, but there were no signs now to indicate that.

"What do you think that says?" asked Ben, pointing at the stark white symbol.

"I don't know, but I might go and have a quick look inside. You guys stay here and keep an eye out."

Without waiting for an answer I ran across the

lawn and up to the corner of the building, stopping and peeking around the corner. There was no sign of movement inside, so with my heart beating fast, I turned the corner and followed the path to the doors.

It was dark inside. I tucked my gun into my belt and cupped my hands around my face as I peered in. The desk was directly opposite the doors and a sign over the reception desk announced Plymouth City Library in brass plated letters. To the left of the desk, a large, arched doorway opened up into a dark, cavernous space. I couldn't make much out at all, just tall shapes I assumed were bookcases. There didn't seem to be much else of interest. I shrugged and, as I was turning to go, bumped against the door, which moved inward slightly before closing softly. It wasn't locked.

I looked over my shoulder. Ben and Paul were still out of sight in front of the building. Knowing I shouldn't really waste time exploring before we went into town, I decided it wouldn't hurt to take just a quick look inside and went in.

Standing in the foyer, I immediately noticed the smell. It was more than just stale or musty air; I detected a subtle undertone of corruption. I turned to the left and walked towards the arched doorway. With every step, the scent of corruption grew stronger and so did my sense of disquiet. The stink was at its most unpleasant at the threshold to the main part of the library, clearly the source of the rot. While it was unpleasant, it wasn't enough to make me turn around.

I wish I had.

As I let my eyes slowly adjust to the dimness, I could make out rows of bookshelves marching like stiff-backed soldiers to the front of the building. I also saw there was something was wrong with the floor. Beginning barely a foot in from the threshold, an assortment of sheets, blankets, and tarpaulins covered the floor. It was uneven and bumpy, the lumps and humps as much as two feet high in some places. Worse were the unmentionable dried stains marring the coverings here and there.

I felt a chill in my bones that had nothing to do with the temperature of the building. I felt frightened as I took a step forward. I knew what was under there, but I had to confirm it. I knelt, and reached out with a trembling hand, grasping the edge of the blanket closest to me, while staying as far away from it as I could.

I took a deep breath and lifted the blanket. It came away with a sticky, ripping sound and revealed its horrible secret. A little girl. I couldn't see all of her ... I didn't want to. Her blonde hair was a pool of gossamer around her head, its vibrancy a stark contrast to the gray, shrunken skin of her face and the black crust under her nose. It was the teddy bear that got me though. It was clutched in her shriveled hands against her chest. A cherished toy that would never leave her side. Tears sprang to my eyes and I suppressed a sob. The bear was just like one my sister, Rebecca, had carried everywhere.

I wiped the tears from my eyes and dropped the blanket back into place. I shuffled along and lifted another. This was an adult male. The crusted black stains on the parchment, like the skin under his nose and around his mouth, showed clearly he had died of the flu, too. I checked another, a woman this time. Same.

The library was now a mausoleum.

I looked around and tried to estimate how many bodies were in the room, but it was impossible. Between the bookcases, the undulating heaps were shoulder high. No, this was not a mausoleum; the word mausoleum implied a respectful burial. This was more a dumping ground. A dumping ground where the dead of Plymouth had been piled like so much unwanted garbage.

I had seen enough. I was about to stand up when the hand fell upon my shoulder.

I jumped in fright, but Ben's soft words calmed me immediately.

"We should go, mate." I nodded, stood up, and followed him out. He didn't say anything until we emerged into the sunlight and fresh air.

"Heavy stuff. You okay?"

"Yeah."

He looked me in the eye for a few seconds, then nodded, satisfied.

5

The further we went without any sign of life, the more I could sense Ben and Paul relaxing. I was still tense; my discovery of the bodies had unsettled me more than I cared to admit. Plymouth was eerie. It had been an occupied town, but now it was clear that it was occupied by nothing more than ghosts. The ghosts of its former American owners and now it's more recent occupiers.

"Is that a tank?" asked Ben, shading his eyes and squinting into the distance.

It was. The large squat vehicle sat smack bang in the middle of the bridge which crossed the river and led into the center of town.

"Should we hide?" asked Paul, with just a hint of worry in his voice.

"No." I walked on. "If there was anyone in it, they would have seen us by now anyway."

For cover, we still walked close to the buildings now lining the street, but as we got closer I could see that even on the other side of the bridge there was no movement.

"Come on. It looks safe, but we'll keep the tank between us and the other side until we get a closer look."

I darted out into the sun drenched road and began to make my way to the bridge in a crouched run, trying to keep the tank between us and the other side. The others were right behind me. When we reached the tank, we spread out behind it, me to the right and Paul and Ben to the left and surveyed the town more closely. Even though the tank was in the middle of the road, there was enough room on either side for a vehicle to pass, so we had no problem seeing all we needed to see.

At the end of the bridge, there was a railway track bisecting the road and further on the right, a new looking, squat three story building. Parked out front were a few military vehicles, but no sign of personnel.

"There's a wreck," said Paul.

I scooted over and joined them. It was an olive green SUV, its front end now sporting a telegraph pole. The impact didn't look like it had been too hard, certainly not enough to kill the occupants, but I could clearly see the shape of the driver slumped against the steering wheel, the white shroud of an airbag draped over him.

"I think it's safe to break cover," I said, standing up.

The car wreck had decided me. Given how things appeared to have been maintained by the occupying force, it seemed unlikely if things were business as usual, the wreck would have been left unattended. It appeared the Professor's virus had, at the very least, driven the enemy from the area around the Drake Mountain facility.

"You sure?" asked Paul, still on his haunches. Ben had already joined me.

"Yeah, come on. Keep your eyes open and your gun ready."

Paul stood up, still looking a little unsure. I didn't think him cowardly, just cautious and I took into account that he wasn't as 'battle hardened' as Ben or I. I gave him an encouraging pat on the shoulder.

We walked across the bridge slowly but deliberately and headed towards the wreck. I put up my hand when we were about twenty feet away.

"Stay here."

I walked the rest of the way alone with my weapon pointed at the vehicle. I was in no danger, not from the occupants of the vehicle anyway. The driver was dead, a messy mix of mucus and blood coating his mouth and chin, his sunglasses pushed askew by the impact leaving one puffy eye exposed. He smelled worse than the desiccated bodies in the library and I covered my mouth with my free hand to try and filter the stench.

I moved to the rear door. Through the window I could see there was another body laying lengthways in the floor well. I was no CSI detective, but the passenger had obviously been lying on the back seat when the impact occurred. I was thankful he was facedown.

I turned and walked back to the others, shaking my head at their unasked question. I motioned for them to continue with me across the railway tracks that crossed the bridge. The squat building was our next destination.

I have to admit I was feeling a little spooked. Whether it was all the death I had so recently come into contact with or the unnatural silence, I'm not sure, but my spider senses as Luke called them were tingling.

We scanned the area as we made our way cautiously to the building. When we stopped on the road out front, keeping a Hummer between us and the entrance, I checked the windows for any sign of movement before deciding to take a closer look.

The doors to the entrance were wide open and I motioned for Paul and Ben to stay back as I crept forward. With my back to the wall, I took a quick peek through the doorway, my gun at the ready. The foyer was empty. There was an overturned chair and some papers scattered on the tiled floor. Opposite the entrance there was a large, unmanned reception desk.

"It's clear; let's go."

We entered. To the left of the desk was an elevator door and, to the right, an entrance to a hallway led deeper into the building. We went to the desk first. On the desk top was a scattering of papers along with a machine gun and a couple of clips of ammo. I picked up one of the papers; the writing was Chinese.

"Looks like they left in a hurry," said Ben, picking up the machine gun and checking it over.

"Yeah," said Paul. "Should we check the building?"

I nodded.

"I want to have a good look around. Do you two want to check this level? I'll go to the second floor."

"Are you sure we should split up?" asked Ben.

"Based on what we've seen, I think we're safe. I'll take the fire stairs. If there does happen to be someone up there, I don't want to be a sitting duck in the elevator."

"The power wouldn't be on anyway, Isaac."

"Oh, yeah," I said, feeling a little stupid.

Ben didn't take the opportunity to tease me. I'm not so sure Luke would have afforded me the same grace, no matter how edgy we were feeling.

"Here, take this," said Ben, offering me the machine gun after he rammed the clip home.

"No, you take it. I'll take your pistol if you don't want to carry it."

He handed the pistol to me and I tucked it into the back of my pants. "Okay, we'll meet back here in ten minutes. Don't take any chances."

6

I went to the fire door to the left of the elevator and pushed it open, stepping in to survey the bare concrete stairs leading up the first landing. The door closed behind me and I found myself shrouded in complete darkness. Not good.

I opened the fire door and went back into the lobby. The other boys were already gone. I dragged a chair to wedge the door open and took the steps two at a time, pausing at the landing and checking I was clear before I moving up to the next floor.

I listened through the heavy door before peering through the small viewing window. It was another reception area with no signs of life. I pulled the door open and eased into the room before closing it gently behind me. The click the door bolt seemed as loud as a gunshot in the (hopefully) abandoned building and I flinched.

I crept to the desk. It was identical to the one on the ground floor. There was a desktop computer and a phone, but not much else. I continued to the entrance of the corridor to the right and looked cautiously around the corner. Big windows ran the length of it, allowing in plenty of light. There were four doors at regular intervals down the left of the hall. I tiptoed to the first one. Again I put my ear to the door. Nothing. My guts were churning as I raised my gun and twisted the handle, pushing open the door.

The stench in the room slapped me like an open hand. I clapped my free hand over my mouth and nose, not daring to breathe the tainted air. I spotted the source of the smell immediately. A bloated body in a khaki military uniform was lying face up on a sofa against the wall to my left. There was a gaping, blackened hole in the top of his head and a spray of dried brains, blood, and bone chips fanning out over the arm of the sofa and the carpet beside the body. The gun lay where it had fallen from the dead man's grip.

To the right, there was an expansive, polished timber desk and above it on the wall was a framed photograph of two men shaking hands. I recognized the Chinese Premier. He was shaking the hand of a General as they stood in front of a column of soldiers. I didn't want to go any further into the room, but forced myself to take a few steps forward and have a closer look at the body.

It was the General in the photograph. I was sure of it, even though the dead man's face was bloated and a corrupt shade of grey, his uniform gave it away. While not quite as elaborate as the one in the image, there were three gold stars on each of the shoulders.

A dead General of the Chinese Army. There was a crust of blood flecked green under his nose and over his mouth and chin. The reason for his suicide was clear.

Across the room, on the far side of the desk was a door. It looked like it had only recently been fitted, the timber frame and wall around it unpainted. I thought briefly of checking that room too, but the smell drove me out. It would lead to the next room anyway and I could just as easily go through the entrance in the corridor.

I burst out of the room slamming the door behind me and ran to the window. I swallowed some deep breaths of the stale but clean air, wishing I could open the window for something fresher. Slowly the sick feeling in my throat dissipated. When I was composed again, I went to the next door.

I opened it cautiously and went in gun first. It had clearly been a small office, but now was furnished with a large king-sized bed. The general had been bunking next to his office. There was nothing else of interest in the room and I moved on. The next room was more interesting. It looked like it had been converted to a makeshift dormitory. There were six bunkbeds, all unmade and messy, and a scattering of clothes and weapons covered the floor and a table in the corner.

I picked up a pillow, removed its case, and began to pick up the discarded weapons. It was quite a haul: two handguns and a machine gun, the same as the one Ben had found downstairs, plus six clips of ammunition. I also found a Kevlar vest. There was no way I could fit it in the pillowcase and I didn't want to carry it, so I put my haul on the bed and slipped it on. There was nothing else of value in the room. I left the room feeling pretty good. If nothing else, we would be going back with weapons and there was hardly a more valuable commodity in the world at that moment.

I was conscious of time and toyed with the idea of not bothering with the other room but decided I would do a quick scan just in case it contained more weapons. There was an overturned chair by the door and the fact there was a deadlock on this one, a few inches above the handle, and clearly not a part of the original door furnishings, intrigued me.

I had to check, right? There was obviously something valuable in there. I tried the handle. It was locked. I thought briefly of trying to shoot the deadlock out, but had a vision of the bullet ricocheting back into my eye.

I stepped back, put down the pillowcase and my gun, and gave the door a solid kick just below the door handle. The wood cracked, but both locks held. I kicked it again and again just below the handle until finally I was rewarded with the sound of splintering. I gave it two more kicks, causing more damage each time, then tried the handle. It rattled and when I leaned against it, the door bowed inward, not obstructed by the flimsier lock, but still held firm by the other.

Luckily it wasn't a solid door. Once the veneer was dented and cracked, I could see corrugated cardboard inside it. I grasped the handle and rammed my right shoulder against the timber door. I had to do it three times before the door crashed open. In the end, it was the door that gave way, as the deadlock actually broke free and fell to the floor. I picked up my gun and scanned the room, a little disappointed.

Before I had broken in, I had imagined the secured room might contain crates of guns and ammunition, maybe even a rocket launcher. What I did find when I looked in was two empty beds. I lowered my gun and was about to turn away when I heard a scuffling sound from the closet to my right. The sound was brief but loud enough to cause my heart to race. I raised my gun and stepped into the room. Hugging the wall, I crept to the closet door and stopped and listened.

I thought I heard a whisper. There was someone in there, possibly two someone's. I decided I would take a risk. I cupped my hand around my mouth, trying to throw my voice so it sounded like I was in front of the door.

"I can hear you in there. I have a gun. Come out with your hands up!"

7

I waited for the crash of gunfire but only silence greeted my demand. I strained to hear anything at all as I stood there waiting. I was at a loss as to what to do. I considered going to get the others, but decided against it. I also considered just shooting through the door. I couldn't; it went against all I stood for, especially not knowing who was in there.

I decided to give one more warning. I stepped in front of the door, assuming whomever was in there didn't have a firearm. To be safe though I got down on one knee to make myself less of a target.

"I'll count to three, if you don't come out I will start shooting through the door. One ... two ...."

Nothing. My heart was thumping in my chest and I paused a little longer before saying, "Three!"

I saw the lever handle of the closet move and I paused, my finger hard against the trigger. The door slowly opened.

"Please don't shoot," said a voice in an American accent.

I stood up and took a step backwards, my weapon still aimed at the closet. A frightened looking teenager with his hands raised stepped out of the closet. He was followed by a bigger boy who didn't have his hands up and didn't look frightened. I was struck by his pale blue eyes. Both of them were about my age and sported shaved heads and a uniform of black pants and a shirt with red piping.

"Stop there."

They both looked underfed and pale. I pointed my gun at the bigger boy.

"Put your hands up, please."

His eyes locked on mine, but he didn't obey my order.

"Ash, please ... put them up," the smaller boy pleaded.

Without taking his eyes off mine, the one who had been addressed as Ash slowly raised his hands. I walked over and warily patted them down one handed. Neither of them were armed.

"You can put your hands down," I said, stepping back in front of them.

They lowered their hands.

"Thanks," said the smaller one, looking relieved.

"What are your names?"

"I'm Danny. This is Ash."

Danny seemed happy and eager to please, now that he had assessed me as non-threatening, but his bigger friend looked indifferent. He was well-built with chiseled features. Danny had a softer look about him and a spray of freckles on his nose and cheekbones.

"You were hiding in there?"

"We heard noise and a crash down the hall," said Danny. "It must have been you ... we've been locked in this room for days. We thought it might be the Chinese coming back."

"I don't think they're coming back. Not for a while at least."

"Why? What's happened?"

"I know you've got lots of questions and so do I. My friends are downstairs waiting though. Let's go down. We can talk then."

I still had my gun in hand and kept a wary eye on them as I directed them through the door. I tensed when the one called Ash paused and looked down at the pillowcase, its opening bristling with weapons. He moved on in short order, but I couldn't shake the feeling he had been tempted. I bent and picked it up as I followed them down the corridor.

Before we entered the fire stairs, I turned to them.

"We're going to walk down the fire stairs to the ground floor. Walk in front of me, and don't try to run or I'll shoot."

It didn't seem right giving orders and making threats to kids my own age, but until I was surer of them I had to give the impression of strength.

"We're not gonna run," said Danny sincerely.

His closet buddy gave me an unreadable look before starting down the steps. When we reached the exit to the foyer, I told them to wait until I gave them the all clear. I didn't want to surprise Paul and Ben and risk an accidental shooting.

I pushed the door open and walked around the chair. Ben and Paul were lounging on sofas when I emerged. They shot to their feet at the sound of the door but quickly lowered their guns when they saw it was just me.

"You're back," said Paul, "We were about to come looking for you. Did you find anything?"

"You could say that," I said. I held the door open and placed the pillowcase on the floor with a clunk. "Don't freak out."

I waved the Danny and Ash into the lobby.

"Whoa!" said Ben, when he saw the strangers. Paul didn't comment but pushed his glasses a little further up his nose, his gaze thoughtful and wary.

"This is Danny and Ash. I found them upstairs locked in a room. I also found a dead General and more weapons and ammo."

I didn't fail to notice the look that passed between the two shaven headed boys.

"General Chang is dead?" asked Danny. He looked surprised more than anything. "What about the rest of them? Are they all dead? We knew they were getting sick and leaving. No one has come for days."

"I'll answer all your questions," I said, holding up my hand and then pointing to the sofa. "But I have some for you first. Sit down, please."

"We under arrest or something?" asked Ash. The first words I had heard him speak, dripping with sarcasm.

"Um, no," I said, a little taken aback at his question. "Just sharing information, I guess."

He looked at my handgun pointedly. That look made me feel like a kid playing cops and robbers. I reached behind me and slipped it back into my belt. He seemed to relax a little after that and they both sat down without any further prompting.

Danny perched on the edge of the seat, almost eager, while Ash slouched back and folded his arms over his chest. I sat on the sofa opposite to them.

"Okay. So I guess the first question is what were you doing in this building?"

Danny answered. "This was their headquarters in the region. General Chang was the regional commander. We were like his assistants, I guess..."

"More like slaves," said Ash, bitterly. "I'm glad that asshole is dead and I hope the rest of the ugly fuckers are too."

Danny paused before he went on; I couldn't help but feel he was frightened of Ash.

"We ran errands and fixed his meals when he ate in his quarters. Also did the cleaning and other stuff they didn't want to waste soldiers on, I guess. But he treated us okay."

He glanced at Ash who stared straight ahead with an ugly, faraway look on his face.

"Mostly, anyway," continued Danny. "Better than the chain gangs anyway."

"Chain gangs?" I asked.

"Yeah, they are more like slaves than we are ... were. They had to clear all the dead out of the buildings and houses." The memory of the dead girl floated across my mind and I forced myself to concentrate on what he was saying. "After that they were working on clean up gangs and stuff, making the town look good, I suppose."

"Where was this chain gang kept?"

"At the hospital. They made the main building into a barracks for the soldiers, but the carpark was fenced in and they put up a few portable buildings. That's where the kids are locked up when they're not working. I've been there once. I can show you," said Danny.

I was thankful for Danny's willingness to share. By contrast, Ash seemed disconnected. I put it down to shock and lack of food, but wondered if there was something deeper behind it.

"Thanks," I said. "That's really good intel. Just sit here for a sec, I need to talk to my friends."

Paul, Ben, and I went to the other side of the room.

"What are you thinking?" asked Ben.

"I'm thinking we need to scope out the hospital and see if ... how many survivors there are. We can't leave them locked up. I'm also thinking we should ..." I was going to say take whomever was willing back to the Valley, but thought better of it. "... well just wait and see what we find when we get there."

They both agreed.

"We're going to need food," said Ben, nodding at the two strangers. "If they've been locked up like these blokes they're going to be starving. I saw a market across the road."

"Okay, we'll make that our first stop. Come on."

I walked back over to the sofa. I had decided not to give too much away about us and the Valley where we had settled.

"I want to talk more, but I think it's important we get to the hospital to see if we can help anyone else. I want to get you two some food and water, too."

"Thanks!" said Danny. "Yeah, it's been a while since we ate. We had tap water in the room, at least."

Ash just shrugged.

"Okay, let's go."

Ben, Paul, and I picked up our gear and collected the two boys on the way outside. I decided that until I knew more about him, I would need to watch Ash carefully.

"Paul, Ben, you take Danny across the road and grab as much food as you can. Make it simple, ready to eat food -- chocolate bars, cookies, that kind of stuff."

"Okay," said Ben. "Come on."

I turned to Ash as the others ran across the road. I smiled and nodded to the nearest Humvee.

"Any chance you know how to start that bad boy?"

He shrugged sullenly. "Could probably work it out ..."

My smile faded as he turned his back on me and walked towards the vehicle. Despite my best intentions, I found myself annoyed at his attitude. The Humvee was unlocked and I went to the passenger side as he climbed into the driver's seat. I had considered putting the weapons in back but decided to hold onto them for the time being.

"Is there a key in the ignition?" I asked.

"No, it doesn't operate by a key."

I craned my neck. I could see a switch on the dash by the wheel. It was a lever on a small black square of sheet metal with three positions, Eng Stop – Run – Start. It was currently pointing to Eng Stop. Ash moved his hand to the lever and clicked it through Run and then to Start. There was a dull click, but the engine didn't start. He let the lever go and it fell back to the run position and an orange light blinked into life above it. He tried it again but there was still nothing. He let it fall back to Run and again the orange light came on. He looked at me.

"Hmm, maybe a dead battery?" I said. "It shouldn't be though; hasn't been that long since they evacuated."

I looked over the other gauges and buttons on the dash but couldn't see anything else that gave a clue as to how to start it. Pity Luke wasn't here, I thought. I was about to say we would try the next vehicle when the orange light above the switch winked out. Did that mean it was ready?

"Try it now," I suggested.

This time when he clicked it into the Start position, the diesel engine rumbled to life.

"Yes!"

My high five was met less than enthusiastically, but I was too happy at our success to let it bother me. I looked down at the automatic gearshift; it looked simple enough.

"Okay, cool, looks pretty easy. Let's help the others."

I pushed my door open and stepped out, looking back at him. He was looking through the windscreen into the distance and for one horrible moment I thought he was going to drive off. If he was considering it, he didn't follow through, and shut the engine off a second later. Feeling uneasy, I met him at the back of the Hummer and opened up the rear hatch. A second later, the door of the store across the road opened and the boys spilled out carrying two bulging plastic bags each.

I smiled when I saw Danny. A chocolate bar protruded from his mouth, gradually getting shorter as he chewed his way through it a bite at a time.

"How did it go?"

"We did great; it was pretty well-stocked," said Paul. "We got some canned stuff to take back, too, although most of it had Chinese labels on it. I guess it will be a mystery box kind of thing until we open them."

Danny struggled and lifted his two bags into the rear of the Hummer then grasped the melting bar in his mouth and finishing it quickly. I pulled one of the bags opened. It was loaded with a variety of candy bars. I picked up the bag and spread it further, offering it to Ash. He didn't hold back, nor did Danny, quickly diving in for seconds. They tore into the packaging like their lives depended on it.

"How long since you guys ate?" Ben asked Danny.

"We had some nuts the day before yesterday. I was beginning to get worried though, the windows were too high up, and we had been working on getting through the door but didn't seem to be getting anywhere."

Paul pulled out a bottle of water for each of them and we waited patiently while they had their fill. Probably not the most nutritious of meals for someone who hadn't eaten in days but we didn't really have a choice. When they were done, I closed the hatch of the Hummer.

"Okay, let's get to the hospital and see if we can find these kids they put on the chain gang."

Everyone started to pile in the back doors, but Ash and I found ourselves both at the driver's door, his hand claiming the handle before mine.

"I'll drive for now," I said, firmly. "Thanks for helping me get it started though."

I braced for an argument as he stared down at me challengingly. He held the door handle for a moment longer, then after an awkward moment or two released the handle and shrugged.

"Sure."

I wasn't sure if he was trying to intimidate me or not, but he did. He intimidated me in a different way than the way Ragg or Chen had intimidated me. Sure, he was big and there was something not quite right about his attitude, but he was also extremely good looking. He was a typical, square jawed, all-American boy and an insecure little part of me couldn't help but worry how Indigo might feel about him if we took them back to the Valley.

I shrugged off my disquiet about him; it wasn't fair to project my insecurities onto him. He had been a prisoner of the Chinese and starved for the last few days, so it was no surprise he might be a bit off. I just wished he could be a bit more like Danny.

I repeated the process Ash had gone through to start the Hummer and the diesel engine rumbled to life again. I exhaled silently in relief, aware he was watching me from his seat.

"Okay, which way?" I asked Danny.

"First, you drive to the intersection ahead, then take a right."

I put the Hummer into drive and put my foot on the gas pedal. The vehicle jerked forward and I eased off the gas before rolling into the roundabout and swinging right onto the main street of Plymouth. We followed it a few hundred yards past empty stores and windows.

"Turn right here, just past the Post Office."

The red brick Post Office was just as you would expect: picture perfect and quaint -- apart from the Chinese flag over the door. I felt a sense of loss wash over me. I guess the others did too. Everyone was silent. Plymouth represented a perfect American town but was strikingly different now, devoid of people and bearing the subtle signs of occupation.

"It's just up this hill a ways and on the left."

I drove the Hummer slowly up the hill, still wary. The town appeared to be abandoned but there were lots of trees and places to hide ... or set an ambush in this part of the town. I slowed the vehicle as we were passing the fire station, its bright red trucks still in their open garage bays waiting for a call that would never come. I pulled to a stop and glanced over my shoulder at Danny.

"How much further?"

"It's the next block."

I made a quick decision and put my foot on the gas. We jerked forward and I swung into the drive of the fire station screeching to a halt and throwing everyone forward in their seats.

"Sorry about that ... bit rusty. We'll go on foot from here. If everything is okay, I will come back and get the Hummer. Danny and Ash, could you bring the bags of food?"

"Shouldn't Danny and I be armed?" asked Ash, looking at me with an unreadable expression on his face.

"Three guns should be enough," I said smoothly, and turned letting him know it wasn't up for debate.

"Fucking jerk."

It was a whisper, but I heard it and I'm pretty sure the others did too. I felt a stab of anger, but chose to pretend I hadn't heard the insult and walked purposefully up the hill.

"No offense, Isaac," said Ben loudly, clapping me on the shoulder. "But that was a bloody uncomfortable ride." Then more quietly, "We'll have to watch that one."

I nodded and felt relief that I wasn't the only one who was bothered by the sullen Ash.

It was late evening now and the shadows were lengthening. We crossed the road and stuck to the sidewalk as we approached the hospital. The carpark of the hospital wasn't as big as I had expected, but it was just as Danny had described.

A chain link fence topped with razor wire enclosed the paved area. At the end we were approaching from, there was a gate with a guard's hut beside it. Inside the perimeter and at the rear were three long, windowless portable buildings. There was no sign of movement, no signs of life. I began to get a sick feeling in my gut.

"Ben, can you take Paul and circle the perimeter? Just make sure there is nothing out of the ordinary and no breaks in the fence. They might have already escaped."

"Sure."

I watched them run across the road with their weapons in hand then turned to watch the buildings for any sign of movement. Nothing. The boys were back in a couple of minutes, also with nothing to report.

There was nothing else to do other than break through the gate and check the buildings.

"Come on."

We crossed the road. I had seen enough so that I wasn't concerned about the Chinese Army anymore, but after my experience in the library, I dreaded what we might find in the buildings.

The gate was secured by a heavy chain and padlock, which drove home the makeshift nature of the 'camp'. If it had been a more permanent structure, I'm sure it would have had electric fences and perhaps lighting. I stepped up to the gate and scanned the fence again to make sure I could see no power boxes or cables. Better to be paranoid than dead.

I gingerly placed my hands onto the chain link, still wary and ready to snatch my hands away. Nothing but cold metal. I pulled the gate towards me, rattling it a little before grabbing the padlock and jerking it. The clinking of the metal was loud in the silence of the ghost town, but I was more concerned about how we would break it.

"Should I try shooting it off?" I asked, as I pulled my gun from my belt.

"Um, I've seen it in the movies, not sure it's

quite as easy as they make it look in James Bond though," said Ben.

"Maybe the fire station has some bolt cutters?" said Danny, sensibly.

"Of course!" I smacked my forehead. "Good thinking, Danny."

He grinned and looked away shyly. I found myself beginning to like him.

"Wait," said Ben, and he went to the guard's booth. After a few seconds, he yelled in triumph and walked out holding a bunch of keys.

"Might take a while," he said, sheepishly. "There a thousand keys on this thing."

"Well, the one thing we have plenty of is time," said Paul.

We stepped aside and Ben began to work through the keys, one by one.

While we waited, I should have talked to Ash and Danny. It would have been an ideal time to try to get to know them and maybe start to integrate them into our group. I was too apprehensive though, the find in the library still haunting my thoughts. I had the unshakeable feeling that once through the gate, we would also find these buildings full of dead Americans.

"Yes!"

It seemed like an hour before Ben finally got the lock open and began to unloop the chain from the gate, but in reality it was no more than five minutes. It fell to the asphalt with a heavy clink and he pushed the gate open triumphantly.

We walked through tentatively. All was silent. I couldn't hear anything from the direction of the buildings. I turned to the others.

"Wait here. I'll check."

"Who died and made this guy leader?" asked Ash, rudely.

"We did, as a matter of fact," I heard the clipped tones of Ben's annoyed voice. "I suggest you shut up."

I approached the first of the buildings, straining to hear any sign of life, my hand sweaty on the handle of my pistol, which was once again in hand. I could hear nothing. There was a set of three metal steps leading up to the door. I paused and took a deep breath before putting my foot on the bottom tread. It creaked and the building shifted slightly when I put my full weight on it. In response there was a squeal from inside. It was cut off so quickly that I wondered if I was hearing things.

"What was that?" Ben called from behind me, his question reassured me I wasn't hallucinating.

With a sense of relief I reached up and pulled the door open. Darkness greeted me ... then a roar and a terrific collision. Suddenly, I found myself flying backwards.

I landed hard, the back of my head cracking against the asphalt as the full weight of my assailant came down heavily upon me. The breath whooshed out of my lungs and I lay there, stunned and gasping, as I tried to breathe. Something whacked me in the side of the face and I could feel a hand scrabbling to release the gun from my numb fingers. It didn't bother me. All I was worried about was trying to breathe and figure out why everyone was yelling. I closed my eyes.

8

I tried to ignore the incessant patting on my cheeks. I felt so warm and comfortable I just wanted to sleep a little longer.

"Isaac! Wake up, mate."

"Isaac?"

I struggled to resist the voices a little longer and then reluctantly allowed myself to float up into consciousness. I opened my eyes. Danny and Ben's concerned faces framed the grey sky.

"Wha --?"

"He's awake!"

I came to my senses and remembered where I was. I immediately tried to sit up, but Ben held me down gently.

"Easy, Isaac, you took a bad knock on the head."

"I'm okay ... I think."

This time he helped me to sit up and my gun fell from my fingers. I abruptly remembered how I'd come to be in the position I was in and twisted my head to look for my attacker. I turned it a little too sharply and the world spun. When it finally stopped spinning, I was able to focus. I saw Paul a few feet away, his gun pointed at the stranger who had charged me.

The boy was big and stocky, wearing a grey jumpsuit. He looked calm but defiant as he held his hands up. Ben helped me to my feet and picked up my gun for me.

"You've probably got a concussion; we'll need to keep an eye on that."

"I'm fine," I said, touching my hand to the back of my head before raising it in front of my eyes. No blood. That was a positive. "How long was I out?"

"A few seconds," replied Danny.

"Has anyone else come out?"

"No."

I looked at the boy from the portable building. "We're not here to hurt anyone. How many of you are there in there?"

Given his size, I was pretty sure it wasn't him who had let out the girly squeal I'd heard before I opened the door.

He didn't answer and just stared at me with a pissed off look.

I walked over to Paul. "If he makes a move, shoot him in the head," I said, in a voice quiet enough not to carry to the buildings, but loud enough for our captive to hear.

I was rewarded with a wide eyed look from the stranger.

"Will do," answered Paul, not sounding at all convincing.

I took a few steps towards the first building. "I know you can hear me in there. We're not here to hurt you. We're here to set you free and give you some food. I need you to step out of the building one by one, with your hands up."

There was no sound from any of the buildings. My head hurt and I was a little impatient now. I stalked to the middle building and banged the metal wall three times with the flat of my hand. Someone inside screamed.

"I said come out with your hands up! No one's going to hurt you. We're American; the Chinese are gone! You can come out."

We heard creaking and movement inside the buildings, before a blonde girl poked her head from the door of the building I had been so rudely ejected from. She looked about thirteen and her face was gaunt and pale and she wore the same grey jumpsuit as my assailant.

"It's okay," I said, smiling and motioning her to come out.

She didn't move but looked at the guy who had jumped me. His mouth was grim, but he nodded. The girl stepped out and was followed by more as the doors of the other two buildings also opened. Pretty soon, we had a crowd of kids standing in front of us. They ranged in age from about ten to sixteen and represented a good cross section of our nation's population ... former population. That was if you didn't notice of the fact there weren't any Asians.

"Ben, keep an eye on them. Danny can you do a count?"

I stepped into each of the buildings briefly to make sure there was no one left behind. The conditions they had been living in were appalling. Mattresses lined the floor with no space for sitting or standing. They told me later the Chinese pretty much made them work from dawn until dusk and, after an evening meal, eaten while sitting on the asphalt of the former carpark, they were locked in the buildings at night.

There was a sink in each of the buildings and a handful of foul smelling buckets. I tested the faucet in the first one and a stream of cool water flowed from it. At least they hadn't gone thirsty. There was no one hiding. I checked the other two buildings, ignoring the stench from both the buckets and the latrine, a simple pit at the corner of the compound which the children had been forced to empty the buckets of waste into every morning.

I stepped out of the last building and squinted in the late afternoon light. My head ached a little, but I felt fine apart from that. It was then I noticed that Ash was gone.

"Where is Ash!?"

My friends, surprised, looked this way and that.

"He was here a few minutes ago," said Paul. "I'm sure of it."

"If you mean the tall dude with the bald head, he lit out of here when you were still on the ground," said the boy who had knocked me out.

"Dammit!" I said.

I thought briefly of pursuing him, but that would leave us shorthanded here, as would sending Paul or Ben. "Not much we can do about it now. Danny, what's the count?"

"Twenty-seven. Twelve girls and fifteen boys."

"Okay, let's give them something to eat," I said, and turned to the crowd of kids. "I know it's getting cool, but I'd like you all to sit on the ground and we'll pass around something for you to eat."

There were no arguments as Danny and Ben began distributing the candy and dried fruits they had managed to scrounge from the store. I walked over to our prisoner.

I was a little distracted. If Ash had absconded with the Hummer, it meant he had the small stash of weapons we'd left in there, too. I knew we could find more, but I didn't like the idea of him running around armed to the teeth. Especially when there was a high chance we might run into him again. I put the thought to the back of my mind. Plenty of time to worry about that later.

"You can put your hands down now."

"Thanks" he said, and lowered his arms gingerly. "Sorry about the hit you took."

I smiled ruefully and held out my hand. "Don't worry, I probably would have done the same thing myself. I'm Isaac."

"I'm Jamal."

"Ben," I called out. "This is Jamal. Can you give him something to eat?"

"No, don't worry about me, I can wait a little longer. Get the rest of them fed first. I'd rather know what you have planned for us?"

Despite our inauspicious introduction, I had a good feeling about Jamal straight away. He was built like an athlete, but I could tell he was a thinker too, and unlike my recent experience with Ash, I felt he was trustworthy instantly.

"You're the leader of the group?" I asked.

"Not really ... I mean we never took a vote or anything. I guess I'm just the oldest and strongest."

"Okay. Well, as for plans, we don't really have any. We didn't know what we would find when we opened the doors. I was expecting the worst. I guess we have some options for you, but that will depend on a few things. Let's sit down over there and have a talk. Danny, give that bag to Paul, you can join in this conversation."

We went and sat down on a bench near the front of the compound. Danny handed two Milky Ways to Jamal as we sat down and, despite his earlier protestations, the boy did a quick job of demolishing them.

"I just want to say I didn't know Ash was going to do that. I'm really sorry, he was always a little weird. He scared me sometimes," said Danny.

"It's okay. I could see he had some issues. Did you have any problems with him?"

Danny shrugged. "Well, he kind of bullied me. Usually after —"

"After what?" I prodded.

"Well, sometimes one of the General's soldiers would come and get him in the middle of the night and take him to the General. He would never say what happened but I knew it wasn't good. He'd be really mean to me for days after."

I thought I knew what had happened and it made me sick to my stomach. No wonder the poor bastard was so screwed up.

"Look," I said to Danny. "I don't blame you for him running off. I should have kept a closer eye on him. I knew something wasn't quite right."

He nodded.

"Where did you all come from?" asked Jamal.

I spent the next ten minutes or so telling them both about our group and the journey that had started back in Rhode Island, what seemed like an age ago. Hard to believe it was less than six months before. I only told them a little about the Valley, unwilling to risk disclosing too much even though I was almost sure they were okay.

"What about you and the rest of them?"

Jamal explained that he and most of the other kids in the encampment had been rounded up from all over New Hampshire, along with a handful from Massachusetts. Neither of us talked about the 'Before Days'-- if he was like me, he also wanted to avoid the pain of those memories.

"What about you and Ash, Danny? Do you know where he was from?"

Danny and Ash had also been in Massachusetts, in Boston itself, when the Flu had struck. He also made no mention of his family or what had happened to them.

"We were in a camp about ten times bigger than this one. Doing the same thing I guess, clearing out the dead bodies in the inner city. I think it was going to be one of their main centers."

"How did you come to be with the General?" I asked.

"I'm not sure really. I mean he picked us, but I don't know why. We were working on Washington Street when his car pulled up. It's like he was inspecting our crew, then pointed at me, and then Ash a few seconds later. Next thing I know, we were put in a truck and driven here to Plymouth. We were taken to the building where you found us and a few days later the General turned up. That's when we were given the uniforms and had our heads shaved. We were told by an English speaking man that we were being given a great honor, and would work for the General as his personal servants.

"I'm pretty sure he was given the job of governing New Hampshire. He had a big map of it in his office, although I couldn't really understand a lot of what was happening, I could see pins and stuff all over it and they were moved occasionally, like they were tracking troop movements, maybe?"

"Strange they would pick Plymouth," Jamal said. "It's not exactly central."

I shrugged. I began to think it was possible the Chinese knew something of the Drake Mountain facility before we thought they did. Anyway, it was a moot point now. The fact was they were gone, for now at least, and we had to get on with things and hope they wouldn't come back.

"So, what now?" asked Jamal.

"That depends. Everyone is free to go their own way or do as they please. The Chinese are hopefully gone for good, but we don't know how for sure how effective the Professor's virus was."

"Pretty effective, I'd say," said Danny.

"Yeah, but the fact is they might only have retreated to the next state and maybe they'll come back when the virus has dissipated. We can't really know. Anyway, I need to double-check with Ben and Paul first, but I'm thinking if anyone wants to, they can come back to the Valley with us."

"You're not worried about strangers coming in and causing trouble?" asked Jamal.

"We have thought about it, of course, but we also know that we can't all live isolated. If we're going to make any sort of life, we need to connect with others. The more of us there are, the stronger we'll be."

"Okay," said Jamal. "Look, I can't speak for everyone here, but not so long ago I thought I might die behind these fences. If you give me a chance, I'll come back with you and work my ass off to be a part of what you're creating."

"Me, too," said Danny.

I nodded. "Okay, I'll talk to Ben and Paul. Can you take over distributing the food?"

Ben and Paul sat down with me on the bench a few minutes later.

"I want to give anyone who wants it the chance of coming back to the Valley with us."

Paul's eyes widened behind his glasses.

"Isn't that dangerous?"

"Maybe," I said honestly. "But it's a dangerous world now and, as Luke said, we'll need to expand to survive. I just wasn't expecting the opportunity to come up so soon."

"I think it's a good idea," agreed Ben. "We can't just leave these kids to fend for themselves. They've been locked up since the invasion; we have to offer, at least."

Paul nodded. "I guess you guys gave me a second chance; it seems like the Christian thing to do."

"I prefer to think of it as the human thing to do," I said. "For the time being, at least, we aren't Americans, Christians, Englishmen, or anything else except survivors and we need to start putting things back together."

"Hear, hear," said Ben.

"Come on.

I stood up and walked to where the kids were

sitting and consuming the food and water we had brought them. Paul and Ben stood supportively beside me. It was funny, even after all I had seen and been through, I still felt nervous as I stood in front of all those kids.

"Hi, everyone. My name is Isaac Race. These are my friends, Ben and Paul. We are part of a bigger group and we've settled in a valley not far from here. We want to ... we would like to offer you the chance to come back with us. To live there with us as a part of a community. I'm sure you realize the Chinese are gone. They may be gone for good or maybe not. For now there's no way to tell, but for us survivors, the best chance for us to keep on surviving is to stick together."

A red-haired girl in front put her hand up.

"You have a question?"

"Yeah, how many of you are there?"

"At the moment there are nine of us."

"That's not many," she said bluntly.

"True, but we've been through a lot. We have weapons and somewhere safe to try and start over. Anyone who wants to come is welcome, all that we ask is that you play by the rules we set down. Anyone who doesn't will be sent away."

No one protested this and there were no more questions.

"Alright, time to decide. If you would like to come with us, please stand up and move to my right."

There was a flurry of movement as nearly

everyone stood up and shuffled to my right. In the end, only a group of three remained seated. Two boys and a girl. They all had sandy-colored hair and were clearly related.

"You sure, Jimmy?" asked Jamal.

"Yeah," said the boy who appeared to be the oldest of the three. "We're going to go home."

"Where is home?" I asked.

"Concord."

I nodded. I remembered Concord well. It was where we had blown up the bar. It wasn't a particularly happy memory. At the time, it had seemed the right thing to do, but I was forever second guessing myself. Could I have done it a different way? According to Luke that ability to hold myself accountable was what made me a good leader, but sometimes I wished I could just make a decision and be done with it, no matter what the consequences.

"Okay, if you're sure --"

I really wanted to warn them off the idea, to ask them to come with us, but who was I to do that? The boy, Jimmy, was my age. He had managed to survive just as long as me and with his siblings too. I was pretty sure he had a fair idea of what to expect.

"Can you drive? It would be quicker and safer if you can take a car. There are plenty in town."

"Yeah, I can. Thanks for the food ... and the offer." He looked at his siblings. "We better get going; we can make some ground before it gets dark."

"And thanks for setting us free," his sister said, as they walked by.

They all high fived Jamal on their way past and he watched them go with a thoughtful look.

"Wait," I called to Jimmy, just before he led the others through the gate. "Here take my gun; I can get another in town."

"No thanks," he said. "Really, we'll be okay. You keep it."

He waved a last time and they went through the gate.

"You think they'll be okay?" I asked Jamal.

"Don't know," said Jamal. "But Jimmy's no dummy, so hopefully yes."

After Jimmy and his siblings left, we put our heads together and decided it would be best to take the whole group back to the headquarters where we could bunk down for the night in relative comfort. We waited for the rest to finish eating and drinking and a few minutes later we were walking back towards the fire station.

"Asshole," said Paul under his breath. "I knew there was something off about that guy."

As I had feared, the Hummer was gone and the stash of weapons with it. Of course, I was angry I hadn't kept a more wary eye on Ash, but consoled myself as we trudged back into town it was not the worst thing that could have happened. How wrong I was.

9

As we walked back towards town leading the straggly troop of grey clad 'refugees', I began to formulate a plan of action for when we arrived back at the abandoned Chinese headquarters. I would send Paul, Ben, and Danny to find more weapons and food while Jamal and I got the rest of the refugees settled in for the night.

I turned to discuss it with Jamal as we turned onto the town's main street and began to pass the Post Office.

"When we get there --"

I was interrupted by a loud burst of rapid gunfire; it echoed through the empty streets. Every one of us fell to the ground. Some of the kids screamed and Jamal quickly shushed them. We all looked around frantically.

"It came from the direction of the bridge," called Ben from the rear of the column.

I didn't waste any time. I quickly ran to the Post Office door. Thankfully, it was unlocked and after quickly checking it was empty, I waved to the others. "Get them in here, quick!"

Jamal joined me at the door, helping to usher his people through the door.

"Don't leave the building until one of us come

back for you," I told him. "Paul, Ben, come with me."

I didn't wait for them to answer, just ran down the street with my gun in hand and my heart pounding in my chest. There was a faint scream, it sounded like a girl, followed by another burst of gunfire that rang out and faded just as quickly. We ran along the sidewalk keeping as close to the front of the shops and buildings as possible.

There was no gunfire for a couple of minutes and finally we could see the roundabout. We heard yelling but couldn't make out the words, except for two that were quite clear.

"No, please --"

The raised and pleading voice was cut off by a final burst of gunfire.

A stampede of thoughts charged through my head, but paramount among them was the fact I would kill Ash as soon as I saw him. This was his doing. It had to be. I tried not to think about Jimmy and his siblings. Over the pounding of our feet; I heard the screech of tires just as we reached the intersection and the stolen Hummer sped away.

"Fuck," said Ben.

It was then, as I started running after Ash that I saw the first body. It was Jimmy's sister, the girl who, just ten minutes or so before, had thanked me for freeing her. I didn't look closely. Didn't want to. I could see she was dead, the middle of her grey top a bloody, ragged mess.

Just a few feet beyond her was the body of her

younger brother. He was face down, shot from behind as he had run away, a bloody trail of wounds ran from his buttocks up to his shoulder.

Their big brother, Jimmy, was on the other side of the road. He was on his back, half in the gutter, half on the sidewalk, his eyes staring lifelessly at the sky. Rage engulfed me and as I ran onto the bridge I began shooting my handgun uselessly at the quickly receding vehicle. I ran on, squeezing the trigger even after I'd emptied the clip.

"You fucking coward!" I screamed, making it halfway across the bridge before I finally stopped and bent over, hands on my knees and my chest heaving as I tried to regain my breath.

I fell onto my backside and sat cross-legged on the bridge for a long time, trying to figure out what we could have done differently. Finally I heard footsteps behind me.

"Are you okay?" Ben asked.

I took a deep, ragged breath and stood up, brushing my hair out of my face.

"Yeah," I said quietly. "I just thought we were done with this shit."

"I don't think we'll ever be done with it, mate. Like Luke says, its human nature."

I didn't respond to that. Couldn't, even if I did want to rage and rail against the unfairness of it. Funny thing was, as tired as I was of all the death and carnage since the invasion, I knew that if Ash suddenly turned that vehicle around and came back, I would kill him right there and then and relish the job.

"Where's Paul?" I asked, turning and starting back across the bridge.

"He went back to tell the others they could come, but said he'll keep them back for fifteen minutes or so to give us time to clear up the bodies."

I put my arm around his shoulders when I heard the hitch in his voice. I sometimes forgot this was as hard on other people as it was on me. "Come on, we better get to it."

We took the bodies one by one into an abandoned house just up from the roundabout. It was a terrible task, and one I feared I would have to do many more times before it was someone's turn to do it for me.

True to his word, Paul led the others to the headquarters around twenty minutes later. No one asked the question I dreaded, even though I saw some of them looking at the bloody patches on the road and sidewalk as we deliberately guided them away.

I could see the shock on Jamal's face as we herded the last of the kids into the building. He clearly knew what had happened without my needing to spell it out. The whole event was more shocking for the fact we'd only been talking to the three victims just minutes before. We talked briefly and I confirmed his worst fears. He didn't cry but was visibly upset, as was Danny. In fact, the shaven headed boy looked to be taking it harder than anyone.

"It's not your fault, Danny," I said putting my

arm around his shoulder as we followed Jamal inside.

I told him the same thing a number of times that night, but he never looked like he fully believed it.

We attempted to provide the rescued kids a more wholesome meal that night. Another visit to the storeroom of the market across the road yielded two boxes of canned baked beans. It was messy; we didn't have anything to eat from or with, so they ate the cold beans inelegantly from the cans with fingers and mouths. There were no complaints; in fact, they wolfed down the food like there was no tomorrow.

Once we had settled the kids into the rooms on the ground floor, Ben, Paul, Danny, Jamal, and I sat down in the foyer and relaxed. Our conversation was productive but constrained. I think we were all still in shock from the recent murders. We told the two boys more about the Valley and our hopes for building it into a home where we could live for the foreseeable future. They expressed enthusiasm and promised to help all they could.

We lay down to sleep after an hour or so, but it was at least another hour before I fell asleep. I ran the events of the day through my mind over and over, trying to think how I could have better handled the situation. Knowing what I knew now, I made a promise to myself I would trust my instincts better from here on in. If I'd trusted them about Ash, then I possibly could have saved three lives that day.

I didn't beat myself up about it too much

longer. At the end, the blame lay with the perpetrator and I hoped one day I would be able to dispense some justice for Jimmy and his brother and sister. When I eventually fell asleep, it was a deep dream filled sleep.

The following morning, we dished up a not so nutritious, but easy, breakfast of M&Ms and Pringles. We had enough for everyone to get at least a handful of the candy and a stack of five Pringles. There were no complaints, even though the carton of Pringles cans we found were well past their expiration date and a little stale. Compared to what they had been eating after the Chinese had departed (they had gotten desperate enough to consume grass and leaves) it was a veritable feast.

I gave Paul the list of 'girl things' Indigo had given me and tasked him with finding them in the drugstore Danny had given us directions to. He took three boys from the chain gang with him. Ben, Danny, and I went to gather more food from the market we had raided the previous day. This time we stripped the shelves of canned and dried foods, things that would last for a long time after we got back. Of course, we stripped it of candy and savory snacks as well, Danny yelling in triumph as he picked up the last packet of Oreos on the shelf.

Even as I smiled at him, I saw his expression of joy change to one of sadness.

"What's wrong, Danny?"

"Do you realize this could be the last packet of

Oreos in the whole United States?"

"I don't think it would be the last, but it might just be the last pack we ever see," I said.

"I love those things," said Ben coming around the corner. "You Yanks have a few strange things you like, like peanut butter and jelly sandwiches — vomit! But I really like Oreos."

"Let's have them," said Danny. "There aren't enough to go around so it's no use trying to share with everyone else."

"Now?" Ben asked, wheeling a cart around from the aisle parallel to ours. He had heard the conversation from the next aisle.

"Why not?"

"Okay, but you need milk if you're gonna have Oreos," the English boy said, reaching into the cart he was wheeling and pulling out a quart of long life milk.

We sat in a circle on the floor and Danny cracked the packet, handing out an equal number of the cookies to each of us. We couldn't dunk our cookies, but were satisfied taking turns chugging the warm milk.

I never did have another Oreo, but have a fond memory of that few minutes sharing with my friends.

We headed back to the headquarters with four trolley loads of goods and Paul and his crew joined us a few minutes later wheeling another four laden trolleys. I noticed the shiny black boots he was wearing immediately.

"Nice boots, how did it go?" I asked him.

"Great," he said, looking happy with himself. "I got everything on the list and a few more things like painkillers, antibiotics, and bandages."

He really had outdone himself. On the way back from the drugstore he had broken into a small hardware store and also brought back a toolbox, flashlights, and boxes full of batteries. He'd even found two big garbage bags of clothes and boots.

"Great work. Okay, let's check these Hummers. I want to go back with at least two."

We definitely lucked out. In the rear carpark, Jamal found a Hummer whose cargo area contained a whole rack of automatic weapons, two crates of ammunition, a box of rocket launchers and another of grenades. He called me over to show me.

"Wow, thank God that wasn't the one Ash and I stumbled across first."

"You can say that again," said Jamal. "There is another one here."

We got in one each and drove the two Hummers around to the front.

We loaded up the cargo area and back seat of the second vehicle with the food and supplies. Then we turned to our last task: transportation of all the kids we had rescued.

Due to a lack of drivers, it wasn't feasible to take more than two Hummers. To take all of the refugees from the camp, we would have needed a whole convoy of them. What we needed was a bus.

We soon had our answer when one of the local kids from Jamal's group suggested his school bus would be able to carry everyone.

"Fantastic!" I said. "Great suggestion ... what's your name?"

"Andrew," the freckle-faced kid said, with a satisfied expression.

"Great, thanks Andrew. Jamal, why don't you take Andrew and go and see if you can get the bus started and back here."

"Sure thing. Come on Andrew."

They began to walk off, and I had a thought. "Jamal, wait!"

He turned back as I was pulling my pistol out of my belt. I lamented the brief flash of fear I saw in his eyes before I turned the handle towards him.

"Here, just in case."

"You sure?" he asked.

"Very sure," I said sincerely, holding his gaze.

"Thanks."

While they were gone, I sent Ben in with Paul and five others to collect all the pillows and blankets they could find and to keep an eye out for any more weapons.

Two hours later, we were loading the kids and bedding onto a tired looking school bus. It was funny, but the sense of excitement that gripped the recently freed kids was infectious. Even I felt it; it was like the excitement and anticipation I felt as a kid when going on a class excursion. Despite the recent tragedy, I found myself happy to be going home.

Our small convoy started off with my Hummer in the lead. Danny rode shotgun with every other available spot taken up by our supplies. The old school bus followed, driven by Jamal, the only one among us who could drive a stick shift. Ben brought up the rear with Paul in the second Hummer holding the weapons, ammunition, and more supplies.

Jamal and I managed to steer our respective vehicles past the tank with no problems. I watched my rearview as Ben drove past it. He was not so successful and the scrape and sparks I witnessed meant he would be in for a decent ribbing about the quality of English driving when we got back.

The trip back to the Valley was uneventful and surprisingly quick now that we were driving. Danny and I chatted happily along the way, carefully avoiding any mention of Ash.

When we drove slowly over the last rise and towards the gates I was gratified to see Luke and Brooke at the gates with their weapons drawn and aimed at us. I waved my hand out of the window, confident he would have the sense to wait until we were closer before shooting. Danny didn't look so sure.

The rest of our group was running up the hill armed and looked more than ready to fight. I looked for Indigo, but didn't see her. I felt a little niggle of worry. It only took Luke a few more seconds more to see that it was us and he quickly put his hand on the barrel of the rifle Brooke was aiming at us and pushed it down toward the ground before calling out to the other defenders. Brooke took his pistol so he could pull open the gates with his good hand. His hook glinted in the sun as he waved us through with a flourish.

I drove through, unable to take the smile of my face.

"Dude!" he said, coming to my window and clapping me a high five with his good hand. "Welcome back. What's with the convoy?"

"Long story," I said. "But we have some new arrivals. I'll fill you in after we get them settled. This is Danny. Danny, Luke."

"Hey, Danny" Luke said.

"Hey."

"Where is Indigo?"

"Don't freak out, dude, she's inside."

"Oh good ... how is your ha-- I mean how is your ...?"

"Stump, dude. You can say it, won't offend me. It hurts like a bitch when the painkillers wear off, but I think it's getting less and less achy each time, which is just as well 'cause I'm running out of tablets."

"Well, we have more if you need them, along with a bunch of other stuff."

"It's okay, I want to wean myself off them. It's good you have more though, and we can always do a supply run to a hospital or something if we run out down the track. Might have to, given this little population spurt."

He stepped aside and I drove through and started coasting down the dirt driveway. The bus and the other Hummer followed us through and I heard Ben tooting his horn.

I pulled to a stop and felt a rush of adrenalin when Indigo opened the door of the farmhouse and ran down the stairs. I jumped out quickly and we embraced like a couple from one of those old black and white movies.

She looked at Danny when we finished kissing.

"Hey," she said to the red-faced boy. He'd gotten out of the vehicle and had been waiting patiently as we greeted each other.

"This is Danny. Danny, this is my girl, Indigo."

"Hey, Danny!"

"Hey," my new friend said shyly.

"I'm so glad you're back," she said hugging me again, burying her face in my shoulder. I pushed her away so I could see her face.

"Why? Is everything okay?"

"Yes, of course. I just missed you, silly."

The bus pulled up with a squeak of brakes and the excited kids began to pile out looking at their new home.

10

After we had unloaded the two Hummers, I called a quick, private meeting with Luke and Indigo. Brooke, Ben, and the rest got the new arrivals settled into the house and began putting together a meal for lunch.

We went into the house and sat on the sofa in the living room in front of the dead TV. I gave my two co-leaders a brief rundown of our trip to Plymouth and how it had ended with the murder of siblings.

"The last we saw of him, he was driving across the bridge with the Hummer and the first set of weapons we found."

"Sounds like an evil motherfucker," said Luke. "Sorry for the language, Indigo, but that goes way beyond just crazy. He gunned them down in cold blood."

"No need to apologize. You're right though; even though the Professor and Ragg were psychopaths, I don't think they were evil to the core. They were sort of molded by circumstance. What this Ash guy did, well, that's just beyond anything ... it's so ... so personal."

"Yeah," I said. "I should have kept a closer eye on him. I knew something wasn't right."

"Don't beat yourself up about it. If you'd stepped in before that, it might have been you, or Ben, or Paul who got killed."

I didn't exactly blame myself for what had happened, just felt guilty that I hadn't been more vigilant.

"Don't worry. I won't beat myself up. So what's been happening here?" I asked.

The rest of the group had managed to get a lot of work done while Ben, Paul, and I were gone. The vegetable garden had been weeded and a system put in place for milking the one cow who was giving milk. They had also managed to find and capture four more of the fugitive hens and a rooster who were all now safely back in the coop. Indigo informed me they had enjoyed scrambled eggs for breakfast that morning.

"Wow, looking forward to some of that ... we didn't exactly eat healthy while we were on the road. We brought back everything on your list though, plus Paul managed to find clothes and some other stuff, too."

"Yeah, he showed me about fifty packs of seeds for vegetables he found in the hardware store."

"He did? He didn't tell me about those; we're going to need everything we can get, I guess."

"Yeah, he already passed them on to Beau," said Luke. "Beau looked pretty happy. I think we've got a real live farmer there. Lucky for us."

"Looks like it."

"Based on how many refugees you brought back, I reckon we'll need everything we can grow and more," said Luke. "We'll have to take up hunting, too. Rabbits will be plentiful and there should be lots of other animals running free."

"Sounds great. By the way, now that we have all these weapons, I want you to set up and be in charge of an armory. You're the most experienced and knowledgeable with weapons, so it makes sense."

"Sure thing," he said. "It was a great haul. There's even a sniper rifle. I claimed that for myself. With this—" he held up his stump, "—I won't be much good in a firefight where I'd have to shoot quickly, but I could be of some use from a distance."

"Awesome."

"What about this killer, Ash?" asked Indigo. "Could he cause us problems?"

"I don't think so. He hightailed it out of there pretty quickly afterwards, but we'll need to be wary anyway. We've got enough people now so we can have two guards at the gate 24/7 and I would also like a patrol walking the perimeter twenty-four hours a day. That'll solve two problems: keeping us busy and making sure we're safe. Not that I'm worried just about him; he's probably long gone. But we don't know who else may be out there. Now that the Chinese are gone, so has any type of law and order."

"Agreed," said Luke. "We'll have to keep a close eye when we send out foraging parties. If this guy is spotted, he should be shot on sight for what he did."

Indigo and I both agreed.

"I also think we should fortify the gate and start reinforcing that fence. It would be next to useless as it is now if we were attacked. We can use metal and timber from the old shed and get more from the neighboring properties."

"Great idea, Luke," I said. "Maybe not the next door neighbor, though. If we end up growing big enough, that's another house and barn we can use to house people."

"Okay," agreed Luke.

"I don't think it's too early to start thinking about having a police force or something either," said Indigo. "It could double as a standing army, you know, a group of us that's always ready to stamp out trouble or in case of attack."

I looked at them: my girl and my best friend. Even though a tiny part of me felt like we were kids playing at make believe, I was thankful I had lucked out and found myself partnered with such intelligent and resourceful kids. I think we all felt that way. We talked for an hour or so, making more plans and ruling in and out suggestions about the way things would work.

11

That afternoon, we had a feast to celebrate our new arrivals and our new home. It was a mix of fresh, canned, and freeze-dried food, but for the kids we had rescued from the compound, it was better than a three course meal in the finest restaurant. Ava piped up at one point and told Paul it was like our very own Thanksgiving.

"You're right, Ava," said Luke loudly. "We should make this date our Thanksgiving."

"I second the motion!" called Beau.

Ever the showman, Luke stood up and rapped the handle of his dinner knife against the table.

"A show of hands, please," he called when everyone had turned to look at him. "Who agrees this day should be our Thanksgiving from now on?"

Nearly everyone put their hands up. Those that didn't raise their hands looked a little bothered. It was clear what they were thinking.

"Don't worry, everybody," I said loudly enough to be heard. "We will still celebrate the normal Thanksgiving as well; this will just be an extra celebration for us."

"Yes, of course," said Luke. "Okay! In my

official capacity as a member of the triumvirate, I declare this day, the third of May, to be the Valley's Thanksgiving Day from this day forward ... that's in addition to the fourth Thursday in November, the Thanksgiving we all know!"

Before lunch, Luke informed me he had given himself the job of keeping track of the date for our little community. He had found a current year calendar hanging in the laundry, so this year would be easy, but he had already started handwriting one for the following year, which he said was a Leap year. I was happy to let him take the job; it wasn't really something I was interested in.

"It's important, dude," he said, perhaps sensing my lack of interest.

After the announcement about Thanksgiving, I saw he was right.

Everyone bunked down in the farmhouse that night, the new people taking up positions on the floor of the living room. It was crowded and warm, but much more comfortable than what they were used to. Before I went to bed, I met in the kitchen with Luke, Indigo, Ben, Brooke, Paul, Jamal, and Beau to discuss our plans for the next day. In no particular order, we decided we would start by assigning one party to dig a latrine and another to clear out the old barn so we could start to turn it into a living space for the new arrivals.

It was a productive meeting. We also elected a

reluctant Luke to be in charge of the security force Indigo had earlier suggested we set up.

"It has to be you, Luke. You know more about weapons and how to use them than anyone I know. We all know you'll be fair and won't try to take over the place like a mad dictator."

When he realized we couldn't be talked out of it, I saw a mischievous glint in his eye as he raised his bandaged stump. "All right, but when Ben finally gets off his ass and helps me get a hook on this thing, I insist you call me Captain ... Captain Hook."

We had a good laugh and after some more quiet conversation, we retired for the evening.

Ben and Luke spent most of the next day working on Luke's hook, while the rest of us oversaw and chipped in with the work that needed to be done.

I took some lunch to Ben and Luke early in the afternoon, curious to see how they were coming along. I found them shoulder to shoulder, standing over a bench as Ben labored over something. They were both dripping with sweat.

"Hey, guys. Brooke fixed you something to eat," I said, craning my neck to see what they were up to.

"Awesome," Luke said, looking over his shoulder at me distractedly. Ben didn't hear me or was too focused on what he was doing to care.

I put down the tray of sandwiches and drinks and moved in for a closer look, standing on tiptoes to peer over their shoulders. Ben was rasping away with a rusty old file at a perfectly formed metal hook.

"You made that?" I asked, wonder in my voice.

Ben stopped what he was doing and smiled.

"Well, not quite. We found it in the back room of the barn. It looks like whoever owned the place was using it as a curing room."

"Curing? Like for meat or something?"

"Yeah, dude, it's a butcher's hook," said Luke, unable to hide the delight in his voice. Clearly, the thought of wearing a butcher's hook tickled him.

He picked up the hook and handed it to me. It was heavy and was about eight inches long. The straight end had been cut crudely, but the rest of the hook had now been filed to a coarse silver finish.

"It was S-shaped, so one hook would go over a bar and the carcass would be skewered on the other end. Anyway, Ben cut about a third of it off. It was a hell of a job, too. He only had a rusty hacksaw blade."

Ben held up his hands, showing me the bloody evidence of his hard labor.

"Ouch," I said. "You better get one of the girls to look at those hands when you're done. Anyway, you should have a break and eat the sandwiches."

Both famished from their hard work in the hot barn, they washed their hands in a trough of water beside the workbench and began wolfing down the egg sandwiches Brooke had made them. She and Indigo had baked the bread fresh in the oven only an hour before and it was delicious. Having power from the generator was a real luxury.

"Wow, these are amazing," said Luke, a crumb or two escaping his overfull mouth. Ben just nodded his agreement.

"How are you going to put it on? The hook, I mean. How will it stay on?" I asked.

"I'm working on a harness while Ben finishes filing it," said Luke. He wiped his hands on his pants and went back to the long work bench, picking up some leather straps which looked like they had come from a saddle or something. "The straps will be attached to the guard that will go over old stumpy here, then run up my arm and over my shoulders."

"Yeah, I'm going to start working on the metal guard when I finish the hook," explained Ben.

"Where will you get the metal for that?"

Ben pointed at an old drum behind me. There was a jagged rectangular hole towards the top rim.

"We already got it, punched it out, just have to shape it into a circle, and clean it up."

"Doesn't sound easy. Good luck with it; can't wait to see it."

I left them to it, pretty sure that, between the two of them, they would come up with something extremely practical. I headed back to help finish clearing the barn of the last of the old machinery which had filled it.

While the house itself had been quite clutter free, whoever had owned the place had made no attempt to clean out the barn. It was a big task but, as the saying goes, many hands make light work. Now that we had made some headway, the doubts I had about converting it to living quarters dissipated.

The barn was huge, with a large open floor space and a couple of rooms to the side. There was also a loft about half the size of the whole ground floor. We had the two Hummers out scavenging the neighboring homes for as many mattresses, pillows, and blankets they could carry or pile on their roofs and, with a bit of luck, we would have bedding for the entire Plymouth group.

By late afternoon, our job was done. We had furnished the loft with an assortment of single and double mattresses. The new kids were excited and happy, several taking the opportunity to engage in a mattress-hopping pillow fight. I didn't stop them, knowing full well it was probably the first time these kids had had any real fun since they had been enslaved by the Chinese.

I didn't need to create rules about boys and girls sleeping separately. Jamal had beaten me to it. He had their respect and friendship from their dark days as members of the chain gang. As we watched them romp, he told me the Chinese had made him a trustee. It was to help them keep the kids in line, of course, but in that role he had become not only a leader, he had also been able to coax privileges and medical treatment from their masters when needed.

"I did the best I could for them. I know it was wrong to cooperate with the Chinese, but we had to make the best of a bad situation ... " he said, sounding slightly defensive.

"I know you did. You don't need to justify it to me, Jamal. I think you did the right thing. I'm sure if you hadn't, some of them wouldn't be here right now."

He nodded.

Jamal seemed happy to maintain the role of authority over the kids who had been in his charge and I was more than happy for him to continue in it for the time being. Earlier that day, when we had first begun clearing the barn, I offered him a bed in the farmhouse. He had refused, saying he wouldn't feel right leaving the kids in the barn while he slept in relative luxury. I was coming to respect him more and more each day, and I definitely felt better knowing he would be there to supervise.

12

The boys did indeed do a good job on Luke's prosthetic. He unveiled it that night. It was just our original group in the kitchen, along with Danny who had said yes to my offer of a place in the house, and Jamal, who was about to head down to the barn for the night. Everyone had eaten by that time and the rest of the new arrivals had already retired to the barn.

An exhausted looking Ben came through the door first. With the poor selection of tools and equipment they'd had, it had literally taken the entire day to craft it to Luke's specifications. The English lad's face and hands were filthy, but his smile shone like that of a proud father.

"Ladies and gentlemen, I present to you Captain Luke Hook!" he announced flamboyantly, directing our gazes to the doorway with his blackened hands.

Luke entered and I was shocked by his appearance. Under the dirt, his face was deathly pale and a sheen of sweat covered his brow. He sheepishly raised his arm in the air displaying the wicked looking hook, turning it this way and that for us to admire.

There were suitable noises of appreciation from all of us and it brought a brief smile to his face.

"How does it feel?" asked Paul.

"It hurts like a bitch. I think it's going to take a while to get used to." He looked like he was going to say something more about it, but instead a look of pain crossed his face and he turned abruptly and left the room.

"Excuse me, I have to take it off," he called over his shoulder. I began to follow him, but Brooke beat me to it, concern etched on her face.

"His stump isn't quite healed yet," explained Ben. "It will take a bit of time for the scar tissue to toughen. He'll be good then."

Ben was right. Luke had a really tough few days and I was thankful Paul had brought back the fresh supply of painkillers from Plymouth.

After a week, Luke was wearing the hook intermittently. From the look on his face when he thought no one was watching, it was clear that it caused him pain.

"He won't take the painkillers anymore," said Brooke, when I asked her about it. "Can you talk to him? He might listen to you."

He didn't.

"No, man, that prescription shit is really addictive; I've just got to get used to it."

I admired his stoicism. Brooke called it stubbornness. Their relationship had developed into much more than a friendship by then, but Luke wouldn't be swayed to take any more painkillers, not even by her.

13

Even as my own relationship with Indigo strengthened and we grew closer, it was interesting to watch our little community begin to develop and the subsequent relationships form. Indigo and I and Luke and Brooke were the only 'official' relationships of our original group, but Ben was spending a lot of time with a girl we had rescued from Plymouth. Her name was Sarah and she was a good match for him. She was a tall, blonde girl, with smarts and a wicked sense of humor. She was originally from Canada, and they took delight in teasing us Americans every chance they got.

None of us talked much about our time in the Drake Mountain facility. When the conversation did turn in that direction, we avoided certain topics because of the dark connotations for Ava and, by connection, Paul.

One night, when we had some rare alone time, I asked Indigo about Ava and her pregnancy. It wasn't long after our first Thanksgiving and Ava was now over seven months pregnant as far as we could estimate. She had only recently opened up to Indigo and Brooke about what had taken place.

"Even though she's pretty private about it, I

think as the birth gets closer, she's been getting more and more worried, so she gravitated towards us a bit."

It made sense. Even though both Indigo and Brooke were just over a year older than Ava, they were the closest thing to mother figures that she had.

"She told us one day when we went for a walk. It was like she was confessing and I think she felt better afterwards. Thank God it was nothing like I had imagined. Actually, I was kind of relieved when she told us. It was all very clinical apparently.

"They gave her something to drink which made her drowsy and took her to an operating room where they put her to sleep. Apparently, the nurses and doctors were very nice to her, but she was still upset, obviously, and no one would tell her why she was there. Anyway, when she woke up, she didn't feel any different, but was frightened out of her mind just by not knowing.

"She went back to the female population after a few days and had begun to put it out of her mind when another girl told her what they had done to her. Naturally, she was upset ... really upset, and they had to sedate her several times. In the end, I think the issue with her not talking to Paul was about the shame of it more than anything else. She felt like it was her fault, like she should have fought them."

I shook my head. The bastards.

"Anyway, all she could do was hope the experiment had failed. The checkups began almost immediately. Every week, like clockwork. When she

SCOTT MEDBURY

missed her period, she wanted to know for sure and hounded them into telling her. After six weeks, they finally admitted she was pregnant. Apparently, she flew into a rage and threatened to kill herself and the baby and had to be sedated again.

"After that, they threatened her that if she ever did anything to harm herself or the baby, they would shoot Paul in the head. The threat worked and she behaved, but her shame and depression kicked in even harder.

"I told her what happened wasn't her fault," Indigo said, wiping a tear from her eye. "And I think by the end of our talk, she began to believe it. I'm so angry, Isaac. I hope the Chinese obliterated Drake Mountain and the Professor. They might have talked themselves into believing it was scientific and for the greater good, but what they did was violate and nearly destroy an innocent girl."

We held each other for a long time.

Perhaps it was a sign, perhaps just coincidence, but two months later, on the 4th of July, Ava gave birth to a healthy little girl. She named her Peace. The circumstances surrounding her conception were forgotten in the joy of that moment and we welcomed our first baby into the Valley. The birth of Peace seemed to herald a new kind of beginning for all of us and we celebrated accordingly with a subdued, but enthusiastic, party.

The baby's arrival was cathartic for Ava. She'd

108

had grave misgivings as she came to the end of her pregnancy, worried primarily that she would not love the baby. In fact, we had all been worried, so much so that Indigo had insisted if Ava couldn't cope, she would take care of the baby.

Paul was even more concerned, confessing to me one night he thought he also would have difficulty loving the baby. In the end, none of us needed to have worried. After the birth of Peace, Ava was transformed. She was a devoted mother from the moment her crying baby girl was put in her arms.

Paul was the same. He burst into tears when we went in to see Ava just a few minutes after the birth and loved his niece without reservation from the moment he laid eyes on her. As we watched the tender scene in front of us, I felt Indigo's warm hand find mine and she looked up into my eyes, as happy as I'd ever seen her. Of course, I was too thick to realize what that look meant.

14

By the time Peace was born, Luke wore his hook full-time and would disappear every morning to a big oak tree at the other end of the farm for what he called his 'workout at the end of the world.'

One September morning, just as the mornings began to feel a little cooler, I was at loose ends and decided to go and see exactly what he was up to. In the distance, I could see him shirtless, darting back and forth at the tree, swinging his hook in quick movements. He had grown his hair long and, with each violent blow, his dark red locks were tossed around his shoulders.

He was an impressive sight. He had bulked up since we had arrived in the Valley, which was not an easy feat given the rations we lived on, and the roped muscle of his shoulders and back rippled under his skin as he attacked the tree with his hook again and again.

I knew he was supplementing his diet with the protein powder he had requested on one of the supply runs to Plymouth and had also been doing lots of heavy lifting, jogging, as well as his daily tree torture routine. The results were evident and, coupled with the fact he'd also outgrown me height-wise by at least an inch, when I stood next to him nowadays I felt a little inadequate.

The solid oak's trunk was scarred with shallow gashes, the fresher wounds displaying the deep honey color of the wood beneath.

"I think he surrenders," I said, after Luke performed another flurry of blows, sending chips of bark and timber flying around him.

He turned, his chest heaving and sweat pouring from his brow.

"Don't worry, he can take it," my friend smiled, and patted the scarred trunk of the big tree. "Isaac, meet Whipping Boy."

"Holey moly, dude, you've done some damage."

"Nah, they're just battle scars. Won't kill him. Want to see my routine?"

"Sure."

Luke crouched in front of the tree before unleashing an attack. The movement of his hook was economical as he attacked it with short, sharp movements which allowed him to rip into the bark an inch or two without actually getting the hook caught. I could hear him grunting with exertion as his attack became more frenzied.

"Killing blow!" he yelled over his shoulder, and his next swing was much heavier than the previous.

The blow obviously didn't work out the way he intended. The hook bit into the timber with a thud, but his arm continued through its arc while the hook stayed where it was, embedded in the wood.

There was a snapping sound as a strap broke and Luke's arm came free of the harness. He nearly toppled over before regaining his balance and looking at his stump, a dumbfounded expression on his face.

I was horrified initially, but the fact that he wasn't hurt, combined with the look on his face, soon had me trying to suppress a giggle. It wasn't to be and, try as I might to contain my mirth, it was too much and slowly but surely my laughter bubbled forth. Luke, far from being offended, joined in. Before long, we were both rolling on the sweet, long grass, gales of laughter wracking us.

When our amusement finally abated, we stayed on our backs looking at the blue sky through the gnarled branches of the oak.

"Things are working out okay for us," he said.

"Yeah. I don't know how we managed to do it, but we did."

"Determination, with a little bit of luck and good management."

"A lot of good luck. The winter will be tough. We have to be prepared for some losses."

By that time, our population numbered sixty-seven. In addition to Peace, we had accepted three more groups of refugees into our community. They were all skinny, hungry kids who had had a tough time and gratefully accepted our rules in order to join the community.

"I don't know, dude," Luke said. "I think we'll be alright. The shelters we've built are sturdy and we've managed to insulate them really well. We've got loads of firewood and plenty of food in the stores."

"I hope you're right."

The latest group of refugees had been brought in only a week before by Jamal, who had been leading a foraging team on a supply run to a little town called Center Harbor. It had been a small tourist town with a supermarket and turned out to be a real treasure trove for food and supplies.

In the supermarket, they had stumbled upon a group of eight kids led by two brothers. After a tense standoff which reminded me a lot of how Luke and I had met Ben and Brooke, the other group had laid down their weapons. Our guys had simply been better armed and there really was no other option. I was thankful for Jamal's calm nature; if he hadn't been leading our group, its possible things may have turned out badly for everybody.

During our debriefing of the new arrivals, we found out they had good reason to be wary. The brothers leading the group, Joe and Brock, told Luke and I they had numbered over thirty just a month ago, but had clashed with another gang of about the same size.

"We were in Plymouth and were on our way out," the younger brother, Brock, said. "Everything there had been pretty much picked over. We were on foot and were about to go under the I-93 overpass when we heard them coming. They were in cars and on bikes. We didn't really have time to hide or anything. Besides, back then we made a habit of talking to people and joining together when we could. That's how we got so big in the first place.

"Anyway, when they pulled up, I could tell there was something off about the leader. But I like to, you know, give people the benefit of the doubt."

I could see tears in his eyes and his brother put a hand on Brock's shoulder.

"Anyway, this guy got out of his Hummer and our friend, Brett, he was like our unofficial leader, waved to him and went over to introduce himself. The guy yelled at him, 'Did I give you permission to speak to me?' Then he ... then he ... he fucking shot him in the face."

Brock couldn't go on; he was too upset at the memory. We gave the two boys a few minutes to gather themselves and then I asked the question I think I already knew the answer to.

"What did he look like?" I asked Joe, a sick feeling in my guts.

"He was ... he was tall, good-looking, and he had these crazy blue eyes."

Luke and I looked at each other.

After Brett was shot, their group had scattered. It had been a cold blooded massacre, but Brock, Joe, and a few of the others managed to escape into nearby trees.

"I don't know how many survived, but we

managed to make it out by going deeper into the forest. If we hadn't, we'd be dead, too."

"Why didn't you fight?" Luke asked, bluntly.

I wanted to cuff him over the ear but the brothers didn't seem offended.

"We were unarmed," Joe said, in a matter-of-fact tone. "Brett made a rule we would never carry guns. He said that's what had gotten the world into the mess it was in in the first place. Once we escaped, well, we changed that rule. We saw that group again a few days later. We were resting on a hill. We were travelling cross-country then and avoiding roads altogether at that point. Anyway, the hill overlooked a small town. We could see that group had set up a camp in the football field of a school. It wasn't a huge group, but there were definitely more kids than just the ones we saw the first time. They had tents and stuff, with a big bonfire in the middle of the field."

"Are you sure it was them? Do you remember the name of the town?"

"Ashland. And, yeah, it was them. I went down for a closer look. I wish I hadn't."

"Why?"

"Near the bonfire, in the middle of the field, they were hanging people. I saw Freddie, one of the kids from our group. They must have—"

"Fuck!" yelled Brock, startling me. "You didn't tell me that. Jesus, poor Freddie."

"Sorry," said Joe. "I thought everyone had been through enough by then. It seemed better to keep it to myself."

"Did you see the leader? The guy with the blue eyes?" I asked.

Joe nodded. "He was like the master of ceremonies. He reveled in it. If I'd had a gun then I would have walked right up and shot him."

I believed him. His eyes had a murderous glint.

"Ash," Luke said.

"Yeah. It could mean big trouble, especially as the first time they ran into him, it was in Plymouth. Where is this Ashland?" I asked.

"I've seen it on the map; it's a few miles south of Plymouth. The name would have appealed to that asshole, like it was fucking named for him."

"Our teams will need to be extra careful when they're doing supply runs from now on. Make sure they have a description of Ash and, if they run into him, they have to know they can't negotiate. He's a killer and they should kill him if they get the chance or get the hell away as quick as they can."

"Yeah, extreme prejudice," said Luke, running his finger over the sharpened point of his hook.

15

Peace was our first baby, but she wouldn't be our last. Our little community grew that first year and continued expanding in the following years. Even though there were more births, refugees were our lifeblood. Most of the people we took in were from nearby. It never ceased to amaze me how many kids actually survived while hiding from the Chinese and in the time after.

As for the Chinese, they didn't come back. We heard rumors and wild speculation from refugees. They had gone back to China. The retro virus had killed them all. NATO had nuked them in retaliation. The scenario most plausible to us was the Chinese had abandoned the East Coast altogether, but still controlled Canada and Central and Western United States.

Given that the Chinese didn't return and no other nations sent aid or forces to help what was left of us, we came to the conclusion the Chinese had simply left the East Coast as a dead zone and the rest of the world had written us off.

It didn't mean the Chinese wouldn't come back in the future, but clearly the territory they had conquered and now had control of was vast. If our speculation about the reasons behind the Chinese attacking the U.S. were correct, they now had plenty of living room and resources.

So life went on for us and it was good. Sure, we had tough times mixed in with the good but, as our group grew bigger, our community spirit seemed to grow, too. No problem seemed too big to overcome.

Over the subsequent years, new arrivals brought other news of the outside world. Lots of it had to be taken with a grain of salt, but most disturbing of all were the tales about a group called the Marauders. It wasn't hard to figure out it was the gang led by Ash. And not so much a gang now as an army. One of our scouting teams confirmed the Marauders had indeed based themselves in Ashland not long after the arrival of Joe and Brock's group and we made a deliberate effort to avoid any contact with them. It was disturbing to know they had flourished even as we ourselves had.

From rumor and eyewitness reports, the Marauders apparently ranged far and wide from their home turf, killing wherever they went. It was lucky we were so remote and away from the highways, but deep down I knew we couldn't rely on luck to keep us safe forever. We strengthened our fortifications and conserved fuel for the small fleet of vehicles we were amassing in case of a forced evacuation. With each new report, our alert levels would rise but then drop to normal again as time passed incident-free.

Eventually, we were finding fewer refugees and thus heard less about Ash and his Marauders.

Within four years, our community had grown to the point we began to discuss the possibility of not taking any more refugees. We were crowded. The buildings we had constructed were ramshackle and the Valley looked like a cross between a rundown trailer park and a medieval village. But even so, we had managed to build a vibrant, peaceful community, with everyone sheltered, fed, and happy.

As a consequence, however, the 813 souls we now numbered stretched our resources to the limit and we knew something would eventually have to give.

The only viable option was moving somewhere else and all of us were reluctant to do that. Indigo and I even more so, given that our son, Max, had been born the year before.

In the 'before days,' becoming a father at nineteen would have been something of a scandal and I have to admit it had come as a shock. It shouldn't have. Indigo and I consummated our relationship barely a month after finding the Valley and we had moved into a room by ourselves not long after. No, I'm not going to give you any details about that first time and how it happened. That's between Indigo and I, suffice it to say it was surreal, magical, and ... brief.

Of course, there were some awkward moments when we announced we would be moving into a room together. Luke and Ben weren't exactly the types to let such a development go without a little ribbing and teasing. Altogether however, our relationship transitioned naturally from a crush to the equivalent of a marriage quickly and easily.

Indigo's initial cluckiness over baby Peace faded pretty quickly when she saw how much hard work a new baby was. And even though we had talked about starting a family from early on in our relationship, it was always understood this would happen somewhere in our future. Birth control was something we were both serious about but, of course, no birth control is perfect and, given the limited supply and life of those products, it was perhaps surprising it didn't happen sooner.

The afternoon I found out I was going to be a father, I had been working in the vegetable garden with Beau. I didn't really have any particular assigned 'job' like most everybody else in the Valley. I tended to go where I was needed and, that day, when Beau told me he had to catch up on the weeding, I offered to help.

We had gone in to the kitchen at lunchtime for the sandwiches and lemonade Indigo had put out for us. Perhaps I should have seen there was something on her mind as she stood against the kitchen bench, her arms folded across her chest and her face thoughtful, but I was totally clueless, even after being told she needed to speak to me in private after lunch.

I followed her to the living room where Brooke

and Ava were sitting playing with Peace.

"I've got a good idea," said Brooke, a look passing between her and Indigo which even I didn't fail to notice. "Why don't we go outside and see the rabbits?"

"What a good idea," said Ava, bending over and scooping up Peace into her arms.

Brooke must have seen the wary look on my face. "Don't look so worried, Isaac," she said, cheekily.

"What's going on?" I asked, after they left.

Indigo sat down and patted the sofa beside her. I sat down. Indigo had a strange smile on her face. She opened her mouth to say something, but suddenly her face crumpled and tears welled in her eyes.

I reached out and grabbed her hand, alarmed. "What is it?"

I watched her struggle to regain control, wiping a tear from her eye.

"You're going to be a dad," she said, before bursting into tears and burying her head in my shoulder.

It's hard to describe what I felt in those first few wonderful, scary moments. The most amazing wave of joy washed over me. It was the most physical emotion I have ever felt, starting with a jolt deep in my chest which emanated like a tide of well-being through the rest of me. I began to cry, too. They were tears of joy, just like the cliché, and I hugged Indigo to me, both of us rocking back and forth, crying and laughing.

"Why are we crying?" I asked Indigo, when we had finally calmed down. "This is really great news! We should be dancing."

"I know! I don't know why. I'm scared, I guess, scared and really, really happy. And I didn't know how you would feel."

"I feel amazing, Indigo," I said, looking into her eyes. "Better than I've ever felt in my entire life!"

She hugged me again.

"Me, too."

16

Our healthy, pink baby boy, Max, was born nine months later. Did it feel strange to be a dad? Hell yes! But it was a wonderful kind of strange. And after he came along, I couldn't imagine life without Max. Indigo was a fantastic mother and the two of us became even closer as we went through the trials of parenthood. After what seemed a long, long time, I suddenly had a family to call my own again.

Even with the overcrowding, the thought of moving my young family and everyone else — when we had order, fresh food, water, and safety — was just something none of us wanted to think about.

Don't get me wrong. Life in the Valley wasn't what you would call easy. In fact, it was hard. Really hard. We lost people through accidents, and illness, and — especially traumatic for Indigo — we even lost a mother during childbirth.

We had to make tough decisions, such as banishing people who turned out to be troublemakers. It sounds harsh, I know, but we didn't have anywhere to jail people and it wasn't worth the trouble to try and rehabilitate them. In the first year, we had come up with a rudimentary code of conduct, which is, I guess, the closest thing to law and order a bunch of kids could have.

That code of conduct was pretty much don't steal and don't fight. If you did one of those things, you got a strike against your name. If you did it a second time, you were out. Anything worse than stealing or fighting resulted in instant banishment. We even had a vote on if, God forbid, anyone committed murder whether we would carry out the death penalty. It was a close vote, but it was defeated, banishment being the preferred option for the majority. I hoped we never had to test that decision.

As decreed that very first night in the Valley, we held an election every year before our Thanksgiving Day. The first two years, Luke, Indigo, and I were reinstalled, unopposed, as the triumvirate. After Max was born, Indigo decided not to run as a candidate and Jamal was elected unanimously to our leadership group of three.

As we entered our fifth year in the Valley there occurred several notable events. On a personal note, Luke and I both turned twenty. Our birthdays were only a month apart and, speaking for myself, it seemed a bit of a milestone. There were no big celebrations or anything, just a feeling we had passed 'officially' into adulthood. It was silly, really. We had been adults for a long time through what we'd experienced.

One morning, not long after my birthday, there came an urgent knocking at our door. Dawn was only just touching the sky. With my heart beating hard in my chest, I ran to the door to find a sleep-tousled Luke jumping from foot to foot. Brooke stood behind him, looking sheepish.

"What is it?" I asked.

"Guess!" Luke said excitedly as Indigo joined us at the door.

"Sorry guys," said Brooke, biting her lip. "I told him to wait 'til breakfast ... "

"We're having a baby!"

Luke leapt into my arms and I staggered back under the weight of his heavy body. I managed to keep my feet until he jumped off and engulfed a delighted Indigo in a gentler bear hug.

"Oh my God, that's so great!" Indigo exclaimed, embracing Brooke after Luke released her.

It turns out they had been trying for six months without telling anybody. I watched Luke standing over Max's cot and felt a warmth for him. I thought it would be great if they had a boy, a playmate for Max, but I knew, boy or girl, Luke and Brooke would be fantastic parents.

On a bigger note, with overcrowding as our top issue, we put a referendum to the people. It was decided by an overwhelming yes vote we would not accept any refugees for the following twelve months into the community. It was a win for common sense and came as a huge relief.

So we moved into our fifth year in the Valley

happy and optimistic about the future. It sounds cliché but, for me, and I'm sure for all of us there, those years in the Valley were the best of our lives. Now that we had the population question settled, it would hopefully be our home for many years more.

Part Three –
Rude Awakening

17

My eyes snapped open. I stared up at the moonlit shadows on the ceiling, wondering if the loud bang had been from a dream I couldn't remember.

"That was a gunshot."

Indigo's soft voice beside me dispelled any doubt that I had dreamed it. I quickly got out of bed and began pulling on my jeans as a burst of automatic gunfire, followed by a distant scream, sent a jolt of electricity through me. We're under attack.

I half-fell/sat on the bed and began to pull on my boots, my fingers suddenly clumsy with alarm. Indigo was already out of bed and carefully bundling up the still sleeping Max.

Bang, bang, bang.

"Quick, you better get him down to the basement. We should get all the girls down there."

"Yep," Indigo said, all business now.

I went to the closet and pulled my pistol and a rifle out and ran to the door. Indigo waited for me there and we kissed as Ben and Luke ran down the hallway past us.

"Come on, lovebird," said Luke, his voice sounding excited and not at all scared. "Those shots came from the gate."

"Be careful," said Indigo.

"I will. Make sure you take some guns down to the basement, and don't come out until you hear one of us give the all clear."

I kissed Max on the top of the head and Brooke arrived carrying a pistol just as I turned to run after my two friends.

"Make sure Luke doesn't do anything crazy!" she called after me.

We flew down the stairs two at a time and ran through the living room, bursting out of the blue door onto the verandah.

It was a dark night and my eyes took a few seconds to adjust as we sped up the hill towards the screaming, shouting, and shooting. More of our people were running from the direction of the barn and the living quarters around it. Some were whooping with excitement, others wide-eyed with fear. It was hard not to get caught up in the excitement, our fear of the unknown balanced by the feeling of camaraderie and safety in numbers.

Luke was a lanky shadow loping ahead of us and he slowed as we approached Boot Hill, a large mound the drive curled around before it straightened and went on to the gates. He turned and motioned all of us to slow and made a chopping motion against his throat with his hook. The whooping of the others slowly subsided as we caught up to him.

The crack of gunfire continued behind the small hill. Luke did a quick headcount as we gathered around.

"You eight," he pointed. "Continue along the driveway, single file, and stick as close to the hill as you can. Isaac, Ben, and I will go around —"

He was interrupted by an almighty crash from the direction of the gate followed by the shriek of metal on metal and roar of an engine.

"Come on, they're through!" yelled Luke.

We ran after him. I can't speak for anyone else, but I felt a righteous anger that someone had dared break through our gate and come at my people. We rounded the hill and began towards the gate. I could make out about twelve shapes on foot, climbing over the debris of the gate and the part of the wall that had caved in with it.

In front of them, speeding towards us, was the vehicle which had broken through our defenses. It was an olive green truck with a heavy metal grate fastened to its front-end and steel plates over its windshield. There were two narrow horizontal slits for the driver to see through and the plating was clearly not part of the original design.

I could see shapes scattered around the wreckage of the gate. Bodies. The bodies of our people. A snarl escaped my lips as I began to shoot at the interlopers. Most of the others with us were not armed with guns but, thankfully, all of the attackers didn't appear to be armed either. Perhaps surprised by our numbers, the invaders began to slow and fall in behind the vehicle which had now slowed to provide cover. I saw at least two invaders return my fire.

One of our guys fell, winged, a quiet kid with blonde hair who had only arrived a year before. My next shot found its mark and the shooter fell, holding his belly. I saw Luke from the corner of my eye. He stopped, half turned, and raised his small crossbow, bracing it on his hook.

The remaining enemy gunman saw Luke and took aim at him, even as he became a target himself. I began to bring my gun around too, when an enraged shriek to my right distracted me. A kid from our side was running at the gunman, a tomahawk raised above his head. The enemy didn't hesitate. He turned his automatic weapon on the kid and let off a burst of gunfire that ceased a split second later when the arrow from Luke's crossbow found him.

Both the invader and the kid with the tomahawk crashed to the ground a few feet apart, the enemy clutching at the bolt in his chest and the kid from our side silent and bloody.

Luke threw his crossbow to the ground. It was only good for one shot because he was unable to reload quickly with his one hand. He pulled a pistol from his belt and began shooting at the slots in the truck's armored windshield. I fired off a shot too, then decided to concentrate on the fighters sheltering behind the vehicle.

I managed to hit one just as the others from our side reached the now almost stationary vehicle, swarming around it and engaging the enemy in vicious, close quarters combat.

From my position to the left of the vehicle, I got a good look at the driver, the glow of the dashboard just enough to display his features. It wasn't Ash. I had no doubt our attackers were from his gang of Marauders, but the driver's eyes were dark, not the eerie light blue of their leader.

The driver snarled as Luke's well aimed bullets pinged around the slit and hit the gas, obviously deciding enough was enough. He aimed straight for Luke, just missing two more of our defenders as they dived out of the way.

Luke waited until the last possible second, then dove out of the way of the two tons of metal death barreling at him. He wasn't quite quick enough; the edge of the heavy grate on the front of the truck smacked his ankle, sending him spinning into the dirt. The driver swung around and rushed back up the hill before pulling up sharply near the fighting, the truck's tires spitting dirt and gravel.

"Grab one of them, Thompson!" the driver yelled.

I broke into a run. The one called Thompson jumped out and snatched one of our smaller boys. I recognized him as Benjamin, a kid originally from Joe and Brock's group. Thompson was bundling him into the passenger door by the time I got there. I couldn't shoot without the possibility of hitting Benjamin, so I ran at them, hoping to wrestle him away before he was taken.

The driver grabbed Benjamin by the hair and floored the gas again, taking off even before his own guy could get back in safely. I dove, grabbing the one called Thompson's leg as he struggled to climb into the moving vehicle behind their captive.

Thompson held on grimly and used his other leg to kick at me. I could hear Benjamin calling out for help, but it was no use. My grip began to slip, the buffeting of the dirt driveway on my legs and feet making it impossible to hold on. Finally, I fell away, rolling several times before coming to a halt. I held nothing for my efforts but a worn running shoe.

I climbed to my feet, remarkably undamaged by my struggle and subsequent fall. I took aim and shot at the rear tires in one last effort to stop the speeding truck. I missed and watched helplessly as the truck careened back over the rubble of the gate and out onto the road.

"Fuck!" I yelled in frustration before running back to the fighting.

I got there as more of our people began arriving. Some of the invaders fled after the truck, obviously not liking the odds, but the rest continued to fight.

I tried to aim at the invaders in the melee, but there was no way I could shoot the enemy without risking my own people. I took the option of firing a shot into the air. It had the desired effect. Everybody froze and I pointed my gun at the face of one of them. It was a kid with a shaved head and freckled face. He immediately dropped his weapon, a short bloodstained axe, and held up his hands.

The other three looked like they were considering fighting on when Luke arrived, his gun and hook glinting in the moonlight. His appearance seemed to help them make the right decision and they also dropped their weapons and put up their hands.

"Get on the ground," Luke screamed at them.

They dropped and Ben began to collect their weapons, an assortment of modified tools. Luke holstered his gun and picked up the axe the freckle-faced kid had dropped.

There was crying and angry shouts from those arriving on the scene as they discovered the destruction of life and limb wrought upon our tightknit community in those few minutes of mayhem.

Now that the heat of the battle had begun to subside, I felt sick and noticed that my hands were shaking. Our one pickup truck arrived, driven by Jamal. He, Danny, Allie, and Beau jumped out and began to help Ben tend to the wounded.

"Danny, Beau, can you make sure these prisoners are tied up and guarded? Luke and I need to inspect the damage," I said.

We ran to the gate. There was no sign of the truck or of the enemy who had run away on foot. It was over as quickly as it had begun, only a trail of death and destruction to mark the enemy's passing.

"They must have had another vehicle waiting,"

Luke said, standing at the broken gates and looking down the empty road. "What are we going to do about Benjamin?"

"I don't know."

Of course I wanted to go after them, to bring him back safely. But we couldn't do that right then. Maybe not at all.

All four of our guards were down and, I feared, dead. They had fought valiantly. We found three dead attackers outside of the wall and another inside the perimeter. We checked our people one by one. Two had been shot and another, a girl I didn't recognize, had a large slashing wound across her neck and down into her chest. The axe.

Her eyes were wide open, staring at the starry sky as if amazed by what she saw there. I gently closed them and felt a cold rage begin to build in me. The last body was that of a young kid of about fourteen. He was lying broken and bleeding in tire tracks left by the truck.

Luke stood back up and faced me, his mouth grim.

"We'll have to work through the night to get the gate back up. We might have to use one of the buses to block it until we can establish something more permanent."

18

We all worked through what was left of the night and by dawn we had managed to repair the wall and bring one of the school buses up to use as a makeshift gate. We had worked with a sense of urgency because, at that point, none of us knew if or when the Marauders would be back with a larger force.

Morning finally dawned as we finished.

Exhausted, I walked down to visit the injured. Jamal had set up some tents and was tending to the wounds of the injured with what passed as medical equipment in our world. At best, that consisted of splints, bandages, antiseptic, and painkillers. Down the hill a ways, Ben and a few of the others were gathering and organizing the bodies of our dead.

Besides the kidnapped boy, Benjamin, we had lost four people at the gate and another two when fighting off the invaders. The boy carrying the tomahawk was alive, but in a very bad way; the bullets had shattered the bones in his upper arm. Jamal shook his head when I looked at him. There were three more injured. One had a broken leg and the other two had more superficial wounds from the fighting.

"They should all be okay if we can keep their wounds clean."

All told, we had killed five of the enemy and had taken four prisoners.

As I walked out of the tent, I heard a heart wrenching wailing. I froze and looked towards the group gathered solemnly around our dead. A girl of about eight was holding and hugging the girl who had been killed by the axe wielder, the blood of the dead girl marring the white sweater she was wearing. Jamal joined me.

"It's her sister."

All of the fear, sadness, and anger of the last few hours hit me like a freight train and I felt the embers of my cold anger flare into something much more powerful. There would be an accounting and it would be now.

I changed course and stalked towards the prisoners pulling out my pistol as I went. Danny stood guard over them, a pistol in his hand. His uncertain look in my direction alerted them and all four looked frightened as I approached.

My fury was as obvious as if my hair had been on fire and they recoiled when I reached them. I leaned over and grabbed the freckled axe man by the collar of his shirt and dragged him over to our dead, his feet kicking in the dust as he tried to escape.

The little girl shrieked when she saw us approaching and fell over her sister as if to protect her. I didn't notice. I swung the killer around, bunching his collar in my hand, squeezing tight as I shook him, his face just inches from the pale face of his victim.

"You see what you've done, you fuck! You murdering fuck!" I spat. I jammed my gun against his temple. "What do you have to say?"

"I'm sorry! Please don't kill me! Please!"

"Too late for sorry, asshole." I forced the barrel harder against his temple and began to squeeze the trigger.

"Isaac!"

Indigo's voice cut through the fog of my rage like a laser through dark night. I froze and looked up.

In her arms, she held Max, my beautiful son. Tears filled my eyes.

"He has to die for what he did," I said simply.

"Not like this, Isaac. Not here. Not now." She nodded towards the grieving, frightened girl in front of us. "It's not how we do things."

"No ... he ... " I struggled to find the words to explain why it had to happen. She walked up to me and gently placed her hand over mine.

"Not like this."

From the comfort of his mother's arms, my little boy looked up at me, his eyes deep pools of blue, and smiled a gummy smile. The fight went out of me.

I let her pull my gun hand away from its intended target. I released the killer's collar and he fell to his hands and knees, coughing and choking for air. Luke came over, his face unreadable and helped the jittery killer back to his comrades.

"Come and rest," Indigo said, tugging gently at my gun hand.

I nodded, tucked my gun into my jeans, and allowed her to lead me back to the house.

19

Indigo persuaded me to have a nap upon our return to the house. It took me a long time to fall asleep, but I eventually did and woke two hours later, fuzzy headed and hungry. I had a late breakfast and called a council meeting to decide what we would do in light of the attack.

Our first decision was quick and easy. Both Brock and Joe had a passion for motorcycles and had kept the four bikes we had obtained over the years well maintained. We sent a team of three on the motorcycles, led by Joe, to monitor the road from Ashland. They were given enough supplies for two days. The bikes were our fastest and least obtrusive form of transport and, if the Marauders did decide to return, I wanted plenty of warning. They were under strict orders not to engage the enemy and to return at speed if they spotted them heading our way.

Next came the question of the four prisoners. It was decided unanimously the four would be tried for murder the following day. The only issue to debate was what punishment would be imposed when ... if we found them guilty.

The worst crimes we'd had to deal with prior to the invasion had been stealing and assault. We hadn't been afraid to make hard decisions and had actually exiled several people from the Valley. That particular punishment seemed to be enough of a deterrent to most of our citizens. We had only debated execution in 'what if' terms.

As I expected, most of the girls were dead set against the idea, all except Brooke.

"We can't just banish them," argued Luke. "What kind of punishment is that? They'll just go straight back to their people and try to kill more of us as soon as they get the chance."

"Luke's right. They've all got blood on their hands. Execution is the only thing that makes sense," said Paul.

"I don't have the answers," said Indigo. "But how can you even think of doing that? Who is going to shoot them? Are you going to pull the trigger, Paul? Luke?"

Paul reddened.

"If I have to, yes," said Luke, resolutely.

"Why are we having a trial at all?" asked Allie. "It seems we've already decided they're guilty."

"But they are!" said Danny. "Isaac, what do you think?"

I looked around the room, my gaze falling on them one by one, until finally coming to rest on Indigo.

"We can't let them go," I said. "And we can't lock them up. Executing them is the only way."

I saw tears in Indigo's eyes. Brooke put her

hand on hers, even though she was of the same opinion as me. I felt like the world's biggest bastard, but we had to do what was right by all of us.

"We know they're all guilty, but we'll have a trial anyway. Our people need to see that we're not just thoughtless killers. We have to talk about what they did and then we have to sentence them to death. Not guns though. I know another way, quick and painless."

20

The next day dawned bright and sunny. Given what we had to do that day, I would have preferred an overcast, miserable morning. I wasn't in a great mood when I woke up. Indigo had been cool towards me when we had retired for the evening, but at least she hadn't rejected my kiss goodnight.

Indigo was silent as we ate breakfast in our room. It was nothing fancy, just some bread and peanut butter we kept in the cupboard in case of hunger attacks. I don't think either of us felt like eating breakfast with the group; certainly she didn't fight me when I suggested eating in our room.

I was feeling lousy, like I had let her down, but I knew in my heart it was the right decision. I washed the last of my bread down with water.

"Well, I better get dressed and go downstairs," I said, pushing my chair away and standing up. Indigo grabbed my hand and squeezed it. Her face was sad, but that simple gesture let me know everything was okay between us. That said, as I got dressed, I still felt there was a heavy black cloud hanging over me. Execution might be the right thing to do, the only thing, but being right didn't make it any easier.

Luke and I had a brief discussion about how we

would conduct the trial and at 9 A.M. we went out onto the verandah. Luke was holding a loudspeaker we had discovered in an abandoned school two years before. It made a horrible screeching sound when he first put it to his mouth and those of us closest to him clapped our hands over our ears. No one giggled though; I wasn't the only one feeling the gravity of the situation.

"Attention, everybody! Please gather in the Square. I repeat, gather in the Square."

Slowly but surely, our people emerged from their quarters or left the jobs they had been doing and began to congregate in front of the raised verandah. We had named that patch of ground the Square and it's where we held all of our community meetings and celebrations, including Thanksgiving and Christmas.

We were silent as we waited for the stragglers to join us. Looking at the sea of upturned faces and listening to the excited buzz of conversation, I was struck by how big we'd grown.

The talk died down as Luke stepped to the edge of the verandah again and held up the loudspeaker.

"People of the Valley, we are gathered here to conduct a trial and pass judgment on the people who attacked our home and killed our people in the early hours of yesterday morning."

"Shoot the fuckers!" someone called from the crowd and it was followed by a chorus of approval and yeahs.

"Quiet down, please," said Luke, holding his

hook up like an unintentional threat.

The crowd slowly fell into silence.

This wasn't to be a trial that would have been familiar to anyone from the before days. There was no judge, no lawyers, no jury. Those of us in the Valley council were essentially judge, jury, and executioner all rolled into one.

Besides the triumvirate (Luke, Jamal, and myself), that year's council was made up of Paul, a boy named Robert who had arrived two years before, Allie, and Danny.

The council was elected every year to govern the everyday running of the Valley. The triumvirate had veto power over any matter, but ever since we'd formed the first council in our second year, we had never had to use it. It was a testament to our single-mindedness when it came to the good of the group.

We were all seated on chairs on the verandah overlooking the crowd. Ben was to act as the court attendant. When Luke settled the crowd and had taken his seat, Ben stepped up and cupped his hands to his mouth.

"Bring out the prisoners!"

The four prisoners were led out by two of our people, members of Luke's security team. The killers had been locked up in the 'compound,' a small enclosure we had built near the trees at the rear of the property. They looked a little worse for the rough night's sleep they had endured. Their hands were tied in front of them and I made a mental note to talk to

Luke about teaching his men to tie them behind in the future.

They were brought to a stop in front of the verandah and told to turn and face us. Three of them had their heads bowed, whether in contrition or in the hope we would take pity upon them I'm not sure. The axe killer looked up at us with defiance. I nodded to Ben.

"You four are charged with murder and injury of the innocent. How do you plead?"

"Fuck off," spat the defiant one.

I felt fury at his attitude and struggled to find something to say. Ben beat me to it.

"I'll take that as a guilty plea," he said smoothly. "Thank you, what about you three?"

The others were more circumspect. Two of them pled guilty quietly; the third started to cry.

"I didn't kill anyone," he blubbered.

"Did you shoot anyone?" Ben asked, no sympathy coloring his voice.

"Yes ... but I only winged him. I hit his arm."

"Right, so you tried to murder him, but your aim was shit?"

"Yeah, but I didn't! He's alive."

Ben jumped down from the verandah and stalked up to the youth, leaning over him threateningly. The boy cringed from Ben's obvious anger.

"He'll be dead by the morning," he said in a low, dangerous voice.

The boy's face collapsed and he began to sob.

"I ... don't ... wanna ... die."

"Shut the fuck up, Singh, goddamn crybaby. They'll get what's coming when Ash comes back."

Ben turned his attention to the freckle-faced axe killer.

"You're a lot braver than you were yesterday."

"Whatever," the boy snarled.

Ben turned on his heels and stepped back onto the verandah and faced them again.

"You stand before our council," he said more formally. "They will decide your fate. How do you vote, council?"

Luke was the first to stand.

"Guilty."

I stood.

"Guilty."

Indigo stood and I held my breath as she paused, looking down at the four.

"Guilty," she said quietly and sat down.

The rest of the council stood, one by one, and delivered the same verdict.

"What is the punishment you've decided?" asked Ben, once we were all seated again.

This time I stood. "The penalty is death."

Still the axe killer was defiant, his teeth bared in a silent growl. The others, even the crying one, took the pronouncement with an air of resignation.

"Take them to the barn."

The two guards moved to take the prisoners

away and I felt myself relax. I turned to Indigo and was about to comfort her when, to my right, Allie screamed. I looked her way reflexively before the sound of scuffling alerted me to the danger behind us. I quickly fell on Indigo, pushing her to the floor as the loud clap of a gunshot sent the crowd scattering. The shot shattered the window we had been standing in front of just a millisecond before, glass spraying over us as we fell to the floorboards.

Later I was told the axe killer had grabbed a pistol from one of the guards and had immediately aimed for me. Only Allie's scream and my quick reaction had saved us.

Call it fate, or luck, or karma, or whatever the hell you want, but that morning, for the first time in two years, I had put my gun holster on. Luke was on his haunches beside me, cursing as he struggled to free his own gun with his good hand. There was another shot and I saw the second guard go down as the killer, his arm around the first guard's neck, backed up, his gun waving this way and that as the crowd scattered behind him.

I didn't hesitate. I got to my feet and aimed at his hateful face. He shot again and I flinched. Thankfully, his aim was less sure this time and I heard a groan behind me. I couldn't waste any more time; I pulled the trigger. I had seen heroes shoot villains over the top of their captives' shoulders many times in the movies, but this wasn't make believe.

Instead of taking the villain in the face, my

bullet struck our own man in the left shoulder.

Fuck! Our man dropped like a stone and the killer reeled back, holding his free hand over his own shoulder. Dumb luck, more than my crappy aim, meant that the bullet had passed through the guard and struck him in the shoulder of his gun arm. It dangled uselessly and the gun he had stolen a minute before dropped from numb fingers. He looked at me, fear now swamping any defiance he still had. He wasn't done yet though.

His head began to turn frantically this way and that. I couldn't risk him taking another hostage. I took a deep breath, calming myself as Luke had shown me what seemed like a lifetime before. I whistled and he looked at me. My second shot took him through the left eye. He fell backwards, the last look on his face: dumb surprise.

There was a lot of confusion over the next few minutes. I'm glad Luke and Ben took charge because I think I was in a state of shock. I sat down on the steps and Indigo sat beside me. The gun dangled from my fingers, as heavy as a brick, until Indigo took it away.

Her warm hand found mine. "You did what you had to."

I could have told her about the fact I had spotted the prisoners' hands tied in front earlier. That if only I'd made them tie them properly when I spotted it, none of this would have happened.

Then again, if Indigo had let me shoot the

bastard the day before, he wouldn't have had the chance to kill again. No, it wasn't my fault. I would put this lapse in judgment behind me, just like I had put others behind me since the Chinese had fucked us over. I had to, not only for me but also for Indigo and little Max.

Beau and Jamal put the guard I had accidently wounded onto a homemade stretcher and took him to the infirmary. Thankfully, he was conscious and didn't appear too distressed. I hoped that was a good sign.

Luke had already covered our latest fatality with a sheet. Another dead kid. It was difficult to think of anyone in the Valley as anything other than kids. Apart from Jamal, who had a few months on us, Luke and I were the oldest of any of the people in the Valley, but no matter what we'd been through or what we were doing, I still felt like a child, albeit one with responsibilities.

The dead boy, Ramsey, was just eighteen. Another marker in our little graveyard. A graveyard which was growing way too quickly. He'd only just been recruited to Luke's security force and I hadn't even known his name before he was killed. I said as much to Indigo, feeling shittier than ever.

"You can't know everyone's name, Isaac. There are too many of us now. Come on, let's go see Max. It'll cheer you up."

I felt like I should stay and help clean things up, but she was right, I needed to see my boy. He was playing happily with Peace when we went into the house.

"Has he been a good boy?" I asked the little girl.

"Yep, he sure has, Uncle Isaac."

"What happened outside?" asked Ava.

While Indigo talked quietly to Ava, I picked up Max and gave him a squeeze, smiling at the gurgle he produced.

"Oh, that's terrible," said Ava.

We sat down there for a while before taking Max up for a nap. We lay for a few hours, Indigo and I, in each other's arms while our little man slept. Just before lunch, there was a knock at the door. It was Luke.

"You okay?" he asked.

"Yeah, what's up?"

"David, the kid who was shot in the arm by the Marauders, died a few minutes ago."

"Oh ... "

"He didn't suffer; he was zonked out on morphine."

"What about the kid I shot?"

"Jamal thinks he'll be okay as long as the wound doesn't get infected. The bullet went through without hitting anything vital."

"Okay. That's good."

"Yeah, um ... listen. We have the three prisoners at the barn. We've been waiting for you. Not really fair to keep them waiting much longer, you know? Death row and all that?"

"Okay. Shit. Of course. Sorry, I didn't even think of it in all the ... excitement. I'll come now."

21

The walk to the barn seemed terribly long on that horrible day.

"So what is your idea? Gassing them?"

I should have known Luke would guess my 'painless and quick' execution method. I nodded.

"Good idea."

"That's me, I'm a real go getter when it comes to killing people."

"Hey," he said, grabbing me on the shoulder. "Remember what they did. What they were a part of. You said it yourself, this is the only way."

I held his fierce eyes for a moment, then nodded and looked at the ground. "I know, man. I'm just a little down on myself for what happened today. I spotted their hands tied in front, but I thought it could wait. I was going to bring it up with you afterwards."

"Dude, I saw it, too. I made a mental note to say something to the boys. That makes me just as guilty as you, right? At least you were able to draw your gun! Mine was stuck in my fucking pants."

I chuckled at his pantomime of the effort he had made to draw his gun, his hook waving in the air as his good hand tugged at the handle.

"Lucky you didn't blow your balls off," I said, laughing for the first time in days. "Fine, you're just as much to blame as me. Stop waving that hook around. You'll take someone's eye out ... probably mine."

I won't describe the execution in detail, but essentially Luke and I banished everyone else from the barn. We took on the responsibility ourselves, unwilling to put anyone else in a position where they had to witness what was to follow.

To say I didn't feel sorry for the boys we loaded into the old Chrysler would be a lie. Two of them broke down when they saw the hose leading from the exhaust to the rear window of the car. It broke my heart. The one who had pleaded his innocence to the murder charge cried and begged for his life as Luke closed the door on him. I saw tears in my friend's eyes and it hit me how unfair this new world was when kids had no choice but to kill other kids.

I think I can speak for Luke when I say it was the most hideous experience of our lives to that point. Taking a life in the heat of battle or in self-defense is one thing, but to have to stand there and watch those three boys die behind the windows of that car, no matter how painless, was monstrous.

Luke held his breath and switched off the car when we were sure they were dead. I opened the big double doors of the garage while Luke opened the car doors to let the noxious gas dissipate and then ran out to join me in the fresh air.

A few of Luke's men were waiting for us

outside. No one said anything when Luke suddenly darted to the side of the garage and threw up his breakfast.

"Give it five minutes. Then take the bodies to the trees out the back and bury them in unmarked graves," I ordered. "Do the same with the one I killed."

I put my arm around Luke's shoulder and we walked back up to the house in silence, neither of us in the mood for conversation.

Late that afternoon, we buried our own dead in the cemetery we had begun in the top paddock of the farm two years prior. A boy named Arthur had been our first casualty. He had fallen out of a tree and broken his neck less than two weeks after arriving. The second had been a girl, Jasmine, who had died from an asthma attack. The third and fourth were the young mother and her baby who had died during childbirth. All of their graves were marked with simple white crosses, their names scratched into them. Senseless deaths in themselves, but somehow less so than the victims of the attack by the Marauders.

What had been four graves now became twelve. Altogether too many for such a tiny and young community. We didn't have a funeral as such, but Jamal asked to say a few words for each of the victims. I was glad. While I had said words over bodies before, these deaths hit me especially hard.

Not because I was particularly close to any of the deceased, but because the Valley was our home and our home was supposed to be a haven. Safety was something I and the others had promised each of the newcomers, and I couldn't help but feel somehow we had failed them.

Jamal's words were well-spoken and poignant and I reflected upon what a valuable part of our community he had become. It was no wonder he had been elected to the triumvirate with Luke and I.

Now that justice had been served and we had buried our dead, we had a hard decision to make. We had put off any decisions until the burials were done and, now that they were, we set a meeting for that night. A meeting where we would have to decide the fate of our whole community.

In the meantime, we had doubled the watch on the wall and armed all of the guards with firearms. After the executions and burials, Luke had gone to the top of Boot Hill with his sniper rifle and had stayed there for hours before finally handing it over to Brock.

He had told Brooke he wanted to give us early warning and an early advantage should the Marauders come back, and that might have been a part of why he had gone up there, but I think he also needed a little solitude after the traumatic events of the day.

22

Indigo and I were in our room an hour before the meeting. Little Max was asleep as we talked in hushed tones about the future of our home.

"Luke wants to stay. It goes against his code of honor to even think of evacuating," I said.

"I know it does. But we have to think of our people, Isaac. If these Marauders come back with a bigger force, they could slaughter us all. You've heard the reports; there could be more than a thousand of them and all killers."

"I know. I've thought about every option. If we stayed and fought, we would probably take out a few of them, but eventually they would overrun us."

"We can't let that happen, Isaac. I think we have to do something none of us want to do. We have to leave the Valley."

We both looked to the cot Ben had built for Max. I knew she was right, but I suspected we would have a hard time convincing the rest of the group. An hour later, we convened in the old kitchen. Indigo and I came in and sat down at the big table. Luke was already there. We were soon joined by Ben, Paul, Jamal, Brooke, Brock, Beau, Danny, and Allie.

Indigo chaired the meeting and jumped straight in. "We can't allow what happened two days ago to ever happen again. This special meeting has been called to discuss measures to keep our community safe. I, for one, can't see how we can stay in the Valley."

Her words were met with some gasps of surprise and Luke looked at her pointedly. To his credit, he refrained from interjecting and let her finish.

"We are outnumbered by the Marauders, outgunned, and they would show no mercy if ... when they attack again. There are more of them and they will overrun us. We need to evacuate and find somewhere more defensible and as far away from Ashland as possible."

Everyone started to speak over one another, only hushing when Luke rapped his hook on the tabletop.

"I can see why you feel this way, Indigo, but I say we fight for what's ours. Don't forget, they have a hostage, too. You're right; they would overrun us if we wait for them to come to us. That's why I propose we go to them before they get a chance. We attack them first and with the element of surprise on our side. We could take them down before they knew what was happening."

"Yeah!"

"Let's do it for Benjamin!"

It was Brock enthusiastically supporting Luke.

Allie disagreed with them loudly, while the others were now more guarded and remained silent. Brooke particularly; she sat quietly, her hand resting on her belly. Luke appeared ready to go on when Indigo spoke over everyone.

"What about Brooke and the baby, Luke?"

She said it quietly enough, but her words were just as powerful as if she'd screamed at the top of her lungs. It was one of the few times I had seen Luke without a ready comeback. Brooke's hand grasped his. He looked at her and she nodded.

I spoke in the awkward silence.

"Indigo's right, Luke. I've been doing a lot of thinking about this ever since ... ever since the breach. You make good points, but the fact is, even with the element of surprise on our side, the Marauders are better armed and might outnumber us as much as two to one. Surprise won't help."

I looked around at them.

"I don't like the idea of leaving the Valley any more than anyone else. But I also think we can find somewhere not too far away that will be easier to defend and perhaps give us the space we need to keep growing. Who we are is more important than where we are."

I gestured to Luke and Jamal.

"In our leadership group, we've been talking about the future, even before the attack, and all of us agreed that even though we've stopped taking in new people, we still have to move eventually. The timeframe we discussed was two years. Right?"

Jamal nodded.

"Yeah," Luke said, looking at Brooke again before addressing all of us. "Sorry, you're right. I just want to punish those fuckers so bad for what they did. But if it leaves the people we love dead, it's not worth it."

"We all want to punish them, Luke," said Indigo. "But Indigo and Isaac are right; it would be a suicide mission."

"For all we know, they already killed Benjamin," Paul said, saying what everyone else feared was true. Brock looked up sharply, but didn't say anything.

Ben spoke then, before things got awkward. "Plus, only about five hundred of our population are able to fight, and even then we would only be able to arm about half of them. The Marauders have at least a thousand, maybe more, and they all fight."

Luke nodded. "All right. I'm convinced. What's the plan?"

"Well we don't have a plan ... yet," I said. "We're going to need to find a location that will house and feed us all, as well as be defensible."

"A town maybe?" suggested Ben.

"Maybe," I said. "Or a city. If there's nothing suitable in New Hampshire, we might have to cross the old border into Massachusetts."

"What about back in the mountains? Maybe Lincoln?" suggested Allie.

Silence greeted her suggestion. Perhaps it felt a little too much like going backwards for us, or maybe it just brought back memories we wanted to stay buried.

"No," Luke said. "I don't want to be chipping icicles off my hook every hour. I think further south would be better."

Allie smiled and shrugged.

"Manchester," suggested Paul.

"Manchester's pretty big. Wouldn't it be too big?" asked Beau.

"Well, it was the biggest city in New Hampshire, but it's not that big. I think its population was about 110,000 people before the attack, so I'm pretty sure we could grow for a hundred years and not fill it up. We could start off populating one part of it and expand as we get bigger."

"Let's look at the map," Indigo suggested.

We went into the living area of the old farmhouse. We had pinned the map of New Hampshire to the longest wall in that room not long after our arrival and had used it to plan forays and scouting missions ever since. In and around Moultonborough and around Plymouth, it was covered in red lines and Xs. Paul traced his finger down the map until it hovered over Manchester.

"Look," said Luke, a tinge of excitement in his voice. "That river, Merrimack, runs through it, but most of the city is on the eastern side. If we could block or blow up the bridge crossing the river there and blockade the other smaller bridges from the western side, we'd only have to worry about one main road in from the north, the 3. Of course, the eastern side would be pretty unprotected, but the only threat we know of for the moment is from the Marauders."

"Yeah," Paul chimed in. "And we could even block the 3 back there where it crosses that smaller river."

We discussed the move well into the night and the more we talked, the more achievable the goal of moving our settlement to Manchester seemed to be. In the end, we didn't even have to vote, it simply became a fait accompli. Of course, that was our core group. We all knew we may have some problems when our decision was relayed to the rest of the Valley's population.

"We should give them the option of staying," said Brooke.

"Yes, Brooke is right," said Ben. "We can't force anyone to come with us. We can only tell them the dangers of staying and hope they make the right decision."

"Agreed," said Luke.

Indigo and Brooke went to bed, content to let us work out the logistics of moving such a big group of people with our limited resources.

"How are we going to do this?" I asked, the enormity of the task suddenly hitting me.

"Easy," said Luke. "We go in a convoy. Our armored Hummer at the head, the three buses and the two SUVs following, then the strongest on foot protected by the other two Hummers bringing up the rear."

"Do we have enough fuel?" asked Jamal.

"Not for all of the vehicles. We'll have to ration it out to make sure the buses have the most and probably the armored Hummer. We should be able to put a good distance between us and the Marauders before any of the others run empty though. I'm thinking it might even be worth taking a longer route and avoiding the 93 to keep as much distance between us and them as possible."

He pointed out a route which would take us east around Lake Winnipesaukee, through Wolfeboro, and back southwest to Manchester.

"We will use more fuel and it will take longer, but in the end it may even be easier to pass. There shouldn't be as many abandoned cars as on the freeways."

We agreed with his suggestion and assigned people to look after the logistics. Luke, Ben, and Brock would be in charge of the armory and weapons and deciding who would be armed with the precious few guns we had. Jamal would take care of fueling the vehicles. Paul would be in charge of supplies, while Indigo, Brooke, and Allie would be supervising the younger of the children. I would oversee the whole operation with the help of Beau.

The rest of us went to bed at 2 A.M. after deciding we would leave at dawn the following day.

That would give us around thirty hours to prepare. As I lay in bed, unable to sleep, a new sense of purpose replaced the last vestiges of anger and sadness at the recent attack and the deaths earlier that day. We just had to hope the Marauders didn't attack before we left. Even if they did, we had our early warning team on motorcycles in place and, in a pinch, we could evacuate in a short time. It would just be much better to leave on our own terms.

23

It's hard to say how I was feeling when we woke up a few hours later. While I was glad to put the last day behind me, beginning what would be our final day in our home had its own kind of melancholy, even if it was tempered somewhat by the anticipation of adventure.

As I ate breakfast with my friends and family, I became more and more enthused by their excitement and optimism. Not only were they excited at the prospect of finding somewhere bigger and more permanent for all of us to live, I think they were almost as enthusiastic about simply doing something different, about having an adventure.

"We should make the announcement," said Luke, as we helped clear away the dishes.

"Yep."

That part I wasn't looking forward to.

We bit the bullet a few minutes later. Luke, Jamal, and I went to the verandah. Luke made his call on the loudspeaker. The crowd gathered a little quicker than usual, perhaps in anticipation of something dramatic like the trial the day before.

I waited until the flow of people into the Square had slowed to a trickle before I began.

"Welcome, everybody."

There were a few claps and whistles, but the overwhelming impression I got was that the audience was still a little shell-shocked from the events of the last few days and were wondering what was coming now.

"I want to start by saying how proud I and the rest of the council are of the way everyone pulled together after the attack and yesterday's trouble. These have been the hardest few days we've had since we settled into the Valley and everybody played their part in fighting off the invaders.

"I guess that brings me to why we called this special meeting. The attack, as bad as it was, really only served as a warning. A warning that things could get much worse. The small force that attacked us belongs to a larger group which calls itself 'the Marauders.' We are of the opinion, the council and I, that they will attack us again and it could happen at any time."

I left that thought with them for a few seconds before I went on.

"The next time, we may not be able to stop them. And so we have made the decision to evacuate the Valley ... tomorrow at dawn."

There was a shocked silence for a few moments and then came the uproar I had expected.

"No!"

"We can fight them!"

"We can't let them chase us out of our home!"

"Please —" I began.

"We're not leaving!"

"No way!"

Even with the loudspeaker, my voice was drowned out. The calls got louder, led by one or two in the crowd who were whipping the rest up, even as others tried to calm things down.

"Everybody! Please, I would like to explain —"

It was no use. They weren't listening and I felt things rapidly spiraling out of control.

I took a deep breath to yell again.

BOOM!

I flinched. The gunshot from my right took me by surprise. I wasn't the only one. The people at the front of the crowd took a step back, stunned into silence. With the smell of cordite in my nostrils, I turned. Luke was still pointing his pistol at the sky, a tendril of smoke curling into the clear morning air.

"You hear that?" he yelled. "If we stay, get ready to hear a lot more of that. Get ready to see your best friend, your girlfriend, or your kid get a bullet through the face. If they're lucky, they'll die in the attack. It will be worse for the ones dragged off by those Marauder assholes, while you —" he jabbed his hook at one of the ringleaders, a heavyset teen who suddenly didn't have a lot to say,"— lie bleeding in the dirt."

He tucked his gun into the waistband of his jeans and stepped up beside me. I could see he wasn't finished and I was happy for him to take over. He certainly had their attention.

"Now, you all know me. You know I don't run from a fight. At first, I wanted to fight, too. But we have to think of the future now." He glanced at the heavily pregnant Brooke. "Truth be told, we are running out of space in the Valley and more than likely would have had to leave within a year or two anyway. We have to go now, a little earlier than we expected, that's all. We can't fight the Marauders. There are just too many of them and they are too well armed. We have to move on and make a new home. Now, please, let Isaac finish."

Luke's intervention did the trick. In his role as head of security, he had become well respected. He was tough but fair and had the added benefit of being big and kind of scary. He was very different to the tall, gangly nerd I remembered from school.

There were no more interruptions as I laid out the plan we had come up with the night before. I was careful not to disclose our destination, just in case there were any who decided to stay. In the worst case scenario, we thought it best to keep that secret until we were on the road. No amount of torture could reveal a secret no one knew.

"Now, we realize this is a shock for all of you and I know you're not all happy about it. I want you to know if you choose to, you are free to stay. We will leave enough supplies for a few weeks and also some weapons for anyone who decides they don't wish to leave the Valley. But, please, I want you to think carefully before you make that decision, especially given what happened a few days ago. Does anyone have any questions?"

"So we leave at dawn?" asked the heavyset boy Luke had put in his place earlier.

I didn't take him to task for his earlier dissention. "Yes, we'll head out at dawn. Anyone who decides to stay needs to let Luke and his team know by sunset."

The rest of the day was frenetic. Mid-morning, we had a brief visit from Brad, one of Joe's motorcycle team. He informed us there had been no sign of the Marauders and grabbed more supplies and refueled before heading back. I told him they were to head back to at dawn unless something happened earlier.

It wasn't easy to prepare over eight hundred people for a sudden evacuation and we were forced to concentrate on big ticket items like transport, food, and weapons. We had to trust individuals would be able select the few belongings they would be able to carry carefully. Not that anyone had a lot anyway. Compared to the 'before days', nearly all of us lived in poverty — that's if you were talking in materialistic terms. Personally, I thought we were better off than a lot of people before the invasion.

As the sun began to set that evening, everything was in place.

"Man, I didn't think we'd get there, but I think we're actually good to go," said Luke as we stood on the verandah drinking a blackberry tea Brooke had brewed for us. It was bitter but palatable.

"Yeah, everyone pulled together really well. I think we should double the guard on the wall tonight. Just in case."

"Agreed. By the way, I had a couple of people working on something. I didn't run it by you because I thought you'd be okay with it."

"What is it?" I asked.

"I've booby-trapped the old bus we blocked the breach with."

"Booby-trapped how, Luke?"

"Well, I kinda made it into a bomb."

"What? Is it safe? We have to go through that gate tomorrow."

"Yes, it's safe," he laughed. "I haven't armed it. I won't do that until everyone else is through the gate. It will be on a hair trigger though; a nice surprise for those assholes when they come back."

"What the hell did you make a bomb out of?"

"Lots of stuff," he shrugged. "Stuff we won't be taking anyway. Fertilizer, chlorine, spare car batteries, that kind of stuff."

"How did you — wait. Do I want to know?"

"Ingenuity, dude, and a good memory for stuff I looked up as a bored kid. Damn, I miss Google!"

"You looked up bomb-making on Google? You're lucky Homeland Security didn't tap your ass!"

He shrugged. "Maybe they did?"

"You didn't build one did you?"

"Are you asking if I was planning a terrorist attack or something?" he smiled.

"No, of course not," I said, raising my eyebrows.

"I was just curious and into science, dude. It's pretty basic stuff though. Lucky most suicide bombers weren't exactly geniuses."

"Suicide bombers?" asked Brooke as she came outside to tell us dinner was ready. "What are you two talking about?"

"Nothing, my sexy, British babe," said Luke, turning Brooke around and encircling her and her belly with his long arms.

"Better be nothing dangerous," she said, turning her head and pecking him on the cheek. "I want this baby to have a daddy, no matter how silly he is."

He winked at me as we started into the house, still hugging.

"Brookster, when have you ever known me to do anything dangerous?"

"Don't worry," I said. "I'll keep an eye on him for you."

Luke released Brooke just before they went through the door.

"Oh wait! I had something else to show you, Isaac. Babe, we'll just be a few seconds."

"Fine. Hurry up, though. It'll get cold!"

"Cool," he said and put his arm over my shoulders, directing me back down the stairs. "I've had some of the kids working on something."

He led me down the stairs and around the side of the house to a stack of something I couldn't quite make out in the dim light until we were closer. They were cutouts. Life-size cutouts in the shape of crouching and standing forms. They were even painted so it looked like they were clothed.

"What do you think? We had to scrape and scrounge for materials, but we got eight finished."

"What are they for?"

"Decoys! Before we head out, we'll position them so they are within sight of the road. They might not be ultra-convincing in full daylight, but hopefully they will make them think we're still here. If they come in the dark, there is a good chance it will fool them. I want them coming through that gate with all guns blazing."

I shook my head in wonder. "Where the hell do you get these ideas from?"

"Oh, this idea? It's nothing," he said. "I got it from the Ghost Army."

I waited but, of course, he was in 'wise one' mode and expected me to ask first.

"Okay, I give up. What is the Ghost Army?"

"Dude, I thought you'd never ask," he laughed. "It was a tactical deception unit the U.S. army had during WW2. They would do things to trick the enemy, like use inflatable tanks and planes to fool the

Germans into believing there was a large force in a particular area, when it was really just a few guys with air compressors and dummies."

I looked at him and nodded, a small smile on my face.

"What?" he asked.

"You know how I've been writing the story of how all of this has happened to us? Well, I think you should start writing a history book of all the weird shit you remember that wasn't even in the history books."

He laughed.

"Dude, it was in the history books; you just weren't reading the right ones. What do you think though?" he asked, gesturing at the cutouts.

"I think it's an awesome idea. Come on, let's go eat. We need to feed that big brain of yours."

We ate a light meal that night as the bulk of the food had been packed into the vehicles. There was quiet talk, but the mood was mostly subdued given that it was our final night in the home we had made for ourselves five years before. We had finished eating and seemed to all be waiting for someone to make the first move to retire for the evening when Ben jumped from the table and told us all to wait right there.

He returned carrying a cardboard box and wearing a big smile. We all craned our necks to see what was inside.

"Nuh uh, no peeking," he said, putting his arm

over the top protectively. He looked at Brooke and smiled. "Now, I was saving this for the birth of my nephew ... or niece, but I figure because this is our 'last supper' in the Valley, we ought to celebrate."

He produced a dusty bottle and with a flourish showed us the label. I knew the name, Dom Perignon. I knew it was a fancy champagne, but most of the others just looked blankly at him. I guess they knew it was alcohol of some kind, but perhaps not its significance in the before days.

We had an unwritten rule that alcohol wasn't allowed anywhere in the Valley. Less than six months before, we had banished a boy for fighting after he had gotten drunk on a six pack of beer he had brought back from a scouting mission.

"It's champagne, people!"

Allie and Ava both wore scandalized looks when they realized it was alcohol.

"You're supposed to look happy, not worried. Don't panic, you won't get more than a mouthful each anyway."

Despite his reassurance, both girls looked to Indigo, who nodded.

"It's okay."

Ben proceeded to pull out a variety of mugs and cups of all shapes and sizes and poured all of us a small portion each.

"Sorry, Sis. In your condition, you can't have any. I'll have your share."

Allie raised a chipped coffee cup to her lips.

"Don't drink it yet!" he yelled.

Allie jumped, almost spilling the precious liquid. Brooke rolled her eyes at her brother as the chastened girl lowered her mug.

"Don't be so bossy, Ben."

"Sorry Allie ... anyway, charge your glasses!" he said, raising his tumbler.

I watched Brooke raise her glass of water and we all followed suit.

"Here's to our five glorious years in the Valley. May our next home be as wonderful to us. Cheers!"

"Cheers!" we all replied.

"Yuck!" said Ava, making a face after a tentative sip.

"I agree," said Allie, laughing after spitting her mouthful back into the cup.

"Savages!" Ben mocked.

We all laughed. I didn't mind the taste. It was kind of bitter, but it had been a long time since I had drank something with bubbles in it.

The mood got a little more upbeat after that. Allie and Ava both finished their cups after some encouragement and seemed to get tipsy on the tiny nip they were given. For that matter, so did Luke. He ended up having Brooke's portion and also Danny's. The smaller boy couldn't be swayed to drink his after his first face-crumpling sip.

"My turn to unveil a surprise," said Luke, disappearing upstairs before anyone could ask. When he came back down, he almost tripped on the last step and both Allie and Ava fell into hysterics as he caught himself.

"What have you got there?" asked Brooke, smiling.

"You'll see," he said, mysteriously.

I could see it was a red plastic box about the size of a briefcase. He went to the small coffee table in the corner and sat it down, opening the lid. It was an old portable turntable. A record player.

"What is it?" asked Ava, walking over to him.

"This is what they used to play music on. Think of it as an old fashioned iPod."

"Really?"

"No," he laughed. "It's better than any iPod ever invented."

He flicked a switch on the side. I heard the built in speakers crackle to life as he lifted the arm and moved the needle over and onto the black disc spinning on the platen.

There were a few crackles and pops and then a repetitive electronic beat began pumping through the tinny sounding speakers. Luke stepped backwards in time with the music, nodding his head in small jerky movements as the beat grew louder.

Ava squealed, laughing when he grabbed her by the hand and swung her to face him, and then he was off, dancing in a hilarious dad fashion as a voice began to sing, "she was born to be ... alive, she was born to be ... alive ... ".

We laughed at Luke and screamed

encouragement to Ava as she began to try and emulate his moves.

"Come on!" Luke called to us over the music, and suddenly Indigo was dragging me into the center of the room, holding little Maxie in the crook of her arm.

Pretty soon we were all up there, the very pregnant Brooke included, laughing, screaming, and dancing by candlelight to that dorky but infectious disco beat, forgetting for a time where we were and where we were heading.

Luke must have played that damn song five times in a row (it was the only record he had managed to find) before, thankfully, the batteries began to die and the artist's voice slowed to an unbearable, horror movie-like drawl.

After the old record player died, we sat around and reminisced for about an hour. We recalled the happy moments rather than the more recent problems and when Indigo and I went to back to our bedroom with Max, I was feeling excited and optimistic about our immediate future. There was also worry, of course, but it had been pushed into the background by the fun that evening.

Indigo had already packed, so after she put Max to bed, there was little to do except go to sleep.

"Good night. I love you, Isaac Race," Indigo whispered, kissing me goodnight.

"I love you, too," I said. We held each other as we went to sleep. It was our last night in the farmhouse; who knew when we would next sleep in a bed?

24

I awoke to the insistent honking of a horn. I sat up, my head sleep-addled. It was coming from the direction of the gate. An engine was approaching the house at speed and I jumped out of bed, snatching my pistol from the bedside table and running out of the room and down the stairs two at a time, barefoot and in my shorts and t-shirt.

"What's going on?" Luke yelled, thundering down the stairs behind me.

"I don't know!" I said, over my shoulder, as headlights lit up the front windows.

With my heart beating furiously, I pulled the door open and ran down the steps as the Jeep from the gate pulled to a stop in a spray of gravel. An excited Brock jumped out and ran over to me.

"We've got trouble! Headlights coming from the direction of Plymouth! Three of them. I think its Joe and the others. But you know what that means."

He didn't need to spell it out. If they were returning at this early hour, the Marauders were on the move. Luke arrived at my side. He was naked from the waist up, the harness and his hook missing for his night's sleep.

"Fuck!" he said under his breath. "We only

needed a few more hours."

"We might still have time, but we need to move now. Brock, drive that Jeep around the Valley and make as much noise as you can. I want everyone up and in the staging area, ready to leave within twenty minutes."

"Yes, sir!"

He ran back to the Jeep and took off, planting his hand on the horn as soon as it was in motion. A sleep tousled Paul and Ben arrived as we turned to head back inside.

"Change of plans," I said before they could ask. "We have to leave now; the Marauders are on the way. I need both of you dressed and out there rounding everyone up. We're leaving in half an hour."

They didn't linger; they knew the gravity of the situation.

"Come on, we need to get the girls and everyone else ready to go. Can you send Beau to bring one of the buses down here?"

"Yep, let's roll."

Joe and the patrol arrived about five minutes after the alarm was raised by Brock. From their vantage near Ashland, Joe, who had been taking the night watch, had seen unusual movement in the Marauders' camp just past midnight.

"I mean, we watched for a while, but it was pretty clear they were gearing up to move, and it was pretty obvious it was for an attack of some sort."

"How many?" I asked.

"To be honest, I didn't stay to find out, but to me it looked like the whole camp was being mobilized. I should have stayed, I mean ... "

"No, you did the right thing. We need time more than intel."

I patted him on the back and sent him to help load the buses down by the barn.

Ten minutes later, we were loading mothers and younger children onto a bus in front of the farmhouse. That included Indigo, Max, Ava, and Peace. Brooke, in her condition, would also ride with them, with Jamal driving. Both Indigo and Brooke were armed with Chinese pistols. Allie was on the bus too. She would ride up front with Jamal and was also armed.

"Take care of my boy," I said, as I hugged Indigo.

"Of course, you take care of you."

I kissed Max on the top of his head and ushered them onto the bus with a lump in my throat. I waited for Luke as he embraced Brooke in a ridiculously long hug. He finally let her go and patted her on the butt with his hook as she walked carefully up the steps. She turned, one hand on her belly, and wagged her finger at him.

"Keep your hook to yourself."

She blew him a kiss before turning and heading into the bus.

We both stood there a moment as the bus

engine rumbled to life and headed up to the clearing we had designated as the staging area.

The whole Valley was a hive of activity, roughly illuminated by the occasional torch and the lights of our vehicles. The two buses by the barn were filling rapidly and up in the staging area I could see the contingent that would be on foot, milling about and ready to move out. For just a second, I nearly freaked out. There were just over seven hundred that would be walking. It didn't take a genius to figure out that if we did strike trouble, we would lose a lot of them.

"Come on," I said to Luke, gathering myself. "I want to get moving now."

We walked up the hill and Luke took the loudspeaker from Allie.

"Open the gates," he called ahead.

One of the guards on the hill jumped in the old school bus and the others went to the front and slowly pushed it backwards, unblocking the opening. The last two buses rumbled up the hill and Ben and Beau marshalled the pedestrians to allow room for the other buses to join the ones carrying the girls.

"Line up five across!" called Ben, as he and Beau walked the line ushering the pedestrians into a marching formation. When they were done, the line curled back down the hill about 150 feet. The rearguard of two Hummers pulled in behind them. We had decided to drain the SUVs for fuel and leave them behind.

"Okay, only one thing left to do," said Luke,

and he walked to the lead Hummer and came back holding a rocket launcher.

"Do you want to do the honors?" he asked.

I shook my head. We had only decided to destroy the house a few minutes before and I didn't think I could pull the trigger.

"Okay."

Luke walked twenty feet or so back towards the farmhouse and checked there was plenty of clear space behind him before putting it to his shoulder. The buzzing of the crowd fell silent until all I could hear was the slight breeze rustling the leaves on the trees to our left.

WHUUUMMMP!

The grenade smashed through the front window and exploded, blowing the rest of the windows out in a bright flash. We all watched as our home began to burn, the kerosene Luke had poured throughout the ground floor doing its job as an accelerant efficiently.

Luke tossed the rocket launcher to the ground and turned around after making sure the flames had taken hold.

I nodded and took the loudspeaker from Ben as we reached the lead Hummer. Ben climbed into the driver's seat as Luke went to the rear of the old bus we had used to block the gate. Together, with the guards, he would push it back into place and then arm the bomb before they all climbed the walls and we moved out.

I put the loudspeaker to my mouth. "Attention, everyone, we're heading out. If anyone wants to stay behind, now is the time to say so." I paused a few seconds, no one came forward. "Good luck and a safe journey to us all."

There was some whistling and clapping as the engines of the Hummers roared to life. I climbed into the lead one and Ben tapped the accelerator as I pulled the door closed. I couldn't resist one last look back over my shoulder at the burning farmhouse as we drove through the gate.

We turned left and slowly drove up the hill. We pulled up after about a third of a mile and got out to watch the progress of our convoy. As the last Hummer was coming through the gates, I saw the yellow roof of the old bus as it was slowly pushed back into place. A few minutes later, our entire convoy was ready to move.

The guards from the gate joined the pedestrian contingent. Luke was picked up by Brock on one of the bikes which would serve as outriders and it raced him up the hill towards us. He waved to the front bus on his way past. I had to admit, from the head of the column, our convoy, or road train, or whatever you wanted to call it, looked pretty impressive. Only a really big force, like the Marauders, would give us any trouble.

Luke arrived and hopped off the bike, giving Brock a pat on the back as he swung the bike around and headed back down the hill.

Luke's cheeks were flushed with excitement.

"Brock will be hanging back and waiting at the top of the hill when they arrive. We need to know whether the booby-trap works and also how many of them there are."

"Good call. Hopefully, they're still an hour or two away. What time is it?"

Luke pulled out the windup watch Brooke had given him for his twentieth birthday. He loved that thing, especially the fact that it had a stopwatch function. He had removed the band and carried it like a pocket watch now. Not a day went by when he didn't pull it out at some point.

"3:37 A.M."

"Okay. Let's head out."

Part Three- Convoy

25

No matter how impressive our convoy looked, it moved slowly. Especially up the hills. We couldn't really have expected anything else considering more than two-thirds of us were on foot. By the time the sun began to brighten the horizon of the eastern sky, I had a sick feeling in my gut. We had made the turn off 25 onto 109 not long after we left the Valley, but had probably only travelled a few miles, three at the most.

"I'm worried we won't put enough distance between us and them," I said to Ben and Luke.

"I know," Luke replied. "We're only as fast as our slowest walkers. We probably could have all been walking and gotten this far."

"Do you think they're in the Valley yet?" I asked.

"Yeah, I'd say they would have planned to attack under cover of darkness. I'd guess they've been there a while now. Hopefully, they take their time to scope things out before they break in."

"Won't they be suspicious of the fire?" Ben asked.

"No, I don't think so," said Luke distractedly. "It should have burned low by the time they arrive.

Hopefully, it just serves to light up my cutouts from behind. About a quarter of a mile down the road, we can hang a right to stay on 109 or we can go left and follow 171."

"What's the difference?" I asked Luke, looking down at the map he was holding.

"Well, 171 is a bigger and better road, but 109 hugs the lake and is probably more direct."

"I'm sure 171 would have been quicker back in the old days, but it's not like we have traffic to worry about. Let's take 109."

We reached the turning point a few minutes later.

"Pull up, Ben. I'm going to give everyone a pep talk. After I'm out, you speed up a bit. We'll drag them along if we have to."

I jumped out with the loudspeaker and walked back along our convoy. As I passed the buses, Indigo spotted me and stood up, pulling open her window.

"Hey there, handsome," she said with a cheeky grin. "Need a ride?"

"My mother warned me never to get into a vehicle with strangers."

"Aww. Fine then, not enough room for you anyway. What are you up to?"

"Just hurrying everybody up. We need to move faster. How is Max?"

"Max is fine. More comfortable than the rest of us, I guess. These seats aren't exactly luxurious." She craned her head to look down the line behind the bus.

"Don't be too hard on them."

I nodded and blew her a kiss as she sat back down. I let the buses pass me and brought the loudspeaker to my mouth. "You're all doing really well. We will stop for a ten minute rest in another hour. For now though, we need to pick up the pace. The Marauders will have reached the Valley by now and it won't be long before they pick up our trail."

Of course, one could live in hope they wouldn't pursue us, but something told me it wasn't going to work out like that. I remembered the bodies of the two brothers and their sister back in Plymouth and I knew there was no way the psycho, Ash, would let us go in peace.

There were a few moans and groans from the walkers, but they all managed to pick up the pace. I decided to walk with them for a while, to show I was willing to lead by example.

About fifty minutes later, I heard the sound of motorcycles behind us. Joe and Brock! I strode towards the front of the convoy as the noise of the engines grew louder. The two riders slowed as they caught up with me, but I waved them ahead, pointing to the lead Hummer. I decided now was the time for a rest and motioned for everyone to come to a halt.

"Okay, everybody. Time for a break. Let's stop here for ten!"

I watched our road train pull up and the walkers slowly begin to sit on the road and the grassy verge as the gate guards handed out bottles of water. I went forward and reached the lead Hummer as Ben and Luke got out and accosted Brock.

"Did it work?" asked Luke, before the riders had even managed to pull off their helmets.

Brock's face was white and his hair wet with perspiration. A fresh red welt stood out starkly on his cheekbone.

"It worked," he replied.

"Tell me, tell me everything. I want a blow by blow account. And what happened there?" asked Luke, pointing to Brock's cheek.

"Wait," said Joe, moving in front of his brother protectively. "Let's go over there."

Ben, Luke, and I walked over to the flat, grassy area Joe pointed out.

"Okay, spill," said Luke impatiently.

"Okay. They got there just under three hours after you left." Brock turned to me. "You definitely made the right call. Their army is huge. Bigger than I expected. They were pretty cautious. The majority stopped about a half mile out and they sent a bunch of guys in on foot. They were in black and armed with bow and arrows."

"They were really cautious," said Joe. "It was an age before they made a move."

"Yeah," said Brock. "It would have been funny, you know, them sneaking up on cardboard cutouts and all, but I couldn't help thinking what would have happened if they'd arrived the day before. Anyway, they set these guys all around, on the hills and by the gate.

"Once they were set, a smaller group arrived but stayed at a distance. I'm pretty sure it would have been the commanders and they had... they had Benjamin. They pushed him to his knees in front of the gate."

"Shit," I said.

Brock swallowed before continuing.

"They called out with a loudspeaker. They were calling out to you, and Indigo, and a few others they knew the names of. Obviously, they had forced Benjamin to give up information about us. They demanded the gates be opened or they would kill Benjamin. Anyway, they gave us five minutes. Some guy counted down the whole three hundred seconds and then, well, the gates didn't open, of course. They — they —"

Joe put his hand on Brock's shoulder. "Don't worry; they get the picture," he said. "I'll tell them what happened next, okay?"

Brock nodded.

"Brock wanted to stop them. I had to hit him to make him quit or we both would have ended up dead."

There was a short pause. Brock didn't seem to hold a grudge against his brother and, after he nodded, Joe continued. "After they counted down and the gates weren't opened, they killed him. It was Ash. He gunned Benjamin down in cold blood, right there in front of the gates with a shotgun."

"Fucking bastard," Ben whispered.

I put my hand on Joe's shoulder as he continued. "They waited for around twenty minutes. I guess until they were sure they weren't going to be attacked. It took them so long to make a move I was getting to the stage I wasn't sure if they were going to, but then someone shot off a flare and I saw the bow and arrow guys."

"Archers," Luke corrected, automatically.

"Right, archers. They began shooting over the fence at the cutouts you set up."

Luke's face remained stony.

"What happened next?" I asked Joe.

"While they were still firing, this massive bulldozer came roaring from further down the road with like two hundred men behind it. It didn't even slow down, just barreled straight for the old school bus. And then boom!" He shook his head. "That booby trap made a real mess of them."

"Good!" said Luke. "How many do you think it took out?"

"Hard to say, but obviously the guy driving the bulldozer. If my count is close, then I'd guess at least ten of the ones coming up behind the bulldozer died and a lot more were injured."

"What then? How long did you stay? Did they turn around?"

He shook his head and the sick feeling in my gut returned.

"I stayed for another half hour. They didn't turn around. They pulled back to regroup, but then came forward again. I think they'd figured it out by then. They sent about a hundred men through once the fires were out. That's when I left."

"Ben, can you grab the map?" I asked. "If they track which way we've gone, we'll need to make a detour. They don't know our destination, so a couple of turns should keep them off our tail."

"Um, there's something else," Joe said. "They have dogs."

"Fuck," said Luke, echoing my own thoughts.

"Okay. Shit. How long did it take for you to catch up with us on your bikes?"

"Ten minutes or so. But I was really hammering it."

"Okay, we've come about five miles. Even going twice as fast as we've been going, they will probably catch us in a few hours. They have some on foot, right?"

"Yeah, about half."

"Even then," said Luke, "there is no guarantee they won't send vehicles to catch us faster. We can't go on at the same pace. What are you thinking, Boss?"

He hadn't called me that in a long time.

"We have to send the buses on ahead, escorted by a Hummer packed with as many guards as we can get in. Once they've reached Manchester, they can leave everyone and just send back the buses for us.

We won't all fit but at least we can evacuate about a hundred more quickly."

"Sounds like it's for the best," said Ben. "The only thing is we don't know what's waiting for them in Manchester."

"True, but we know what's behind us. We just have to hope they'll be alright. Come on, let's break the news."

We went onto the lead bus and told them the changes of plans. Of course, neither Indigo nor Brooke was happy with the idea, but they couldn't argue with the logic.

We said another goodbye, this one more poignant, and I kissed my wife and my son goodbye, holding both of them in my arms for the longest time. I saw tears in Brooke's eyes as Luke turned away from her. I vowed silently to bring him back safely to her.

"Can we send Ben with them?" Luke asked. "You know he'd rather die than let anything happen to the girls."

"Yeah, I thought the same myself. Ben, Danny, and Jamal will drive the buses to Manchester. I want all of them armed. See if you can stack the Hummer with at least six of your guys and the weapons they'll need. Paul can drive. Hurry."

Within a few minutes, we were again waving goodbye to the bus. For real this time. Tears stung my eyes when Indigo held Max up to the window and waved his chubby little arm. I waved until the bus was out of sight, acutely aware it might be the last time I saw my wife and son.

26

After the buses departed, I took the loudspeaker from the remaining Hummer. I didn't hold back. I told everyone the situation in plain terms, driving home the fact we had to move even more quickly now. I scanned their faces as I spoke. The majority were armed with homemade clubs, pickaxe handles, and other tools. I knew they would give a good account of themselves if they ever got the opportunity to get into close quarters fighting.

It was a big 'if' though, given the firepower of our enemy. If the Marauders caught up with us, most of our group would be slaughtered before raising a weapon. Our only hope was to get to Manchester without engaging. At least there we would have a chance.

I sent Beau and Brock ahead on bikes to set the pace at the head of the column. I didn't think Brock should go back to track the Marauders after what happened to Benjamin. He seemed more rash and likely to do something foolish than Joe.

I sent Joe and the other rider, Brad, back to monitor the progress of the Marauders. On the small chance they found the enemy had turned back, they were to notify us immediately. Other than that, they were to stay ahead of the Marauders by a mile or so until we were in sight. At that time, they would ride forward as fast as they could to warn us so we could ready ourselves for battle.

Along the way, Brad was to leave Joe and report to us every half hour. I gave them a handwritten map with the turns we would be taking. When I thought about it clearly, the fact the Marauders had dogs might actually be a mixed blessing because, to track us, they would only be able to go as fast as the animals would allow.

We set off at a brisk pace. The bikes lead those on foot and unarmed first, followed by Luke and me bringing up the armed contingent. The remaining two Hummers brought up the rear.

We made much better ground now that Beau and Brock were at the head of the column. Within twenty minutes, we reached the town of Wolfboro. It was right on the water and the land around it was level and green. As we walked through it, I could see that in its time it would have been a pretty little town, but now it was just plain creepy. A ghost town. It only took a few minutes to pass through the town and not far past it we turned onto 28.

"Okay, about a half mile ahead we should reach a town called Alton —"

Luke was interrupted by the sound of a motorcycle behind us. We looked at each other before turning around. It was Brad. I watched him approach with some trepidation. Would it be good news or bad? He hopped off his bike and wheeled it along as we continued to walk.

"Hey," he said, without taking his helmet off. "They didn't turn back. They're following, not too fast, but faster than you guys."

"How many?"

"All of them."

I nodded.

"Dogs?"

"Yeah."

"Okay, how far behind?"

"Roughly about two-and-a-half miles."

"Thanks. You can go back. See you in half an hour."

As he sped off, I looked at Luke.

"They've gained a mile on us already."

"Yeah," he said. "I think we'll have to make a stand before too long."

"Let's worry about that later."

We pushed on and hadn't quite reached Alton when Brad caught up with us again. The sun was higher in the sky now and my stomach growled.

"How far now?" I asked.

"I don't think they made as much ground this time. I think just over two miles."

Still too close. We sent him on his way again and I told him not to come back until they had closed the distance to a mile-and-a-half.

We stopped briefly in Alton to eat and drink and were back on the move within ten minutes. I had taken a look at Luke's map, dismayed to see that Alton was barely a third of the way to our destination. Things were looking grimmer by the minute.

"We have to start thinking about where we want to make a stand," Luke said as we walked out of town.

"Okay. Any suggestions?"

"Yeah, I've already thought about it."

"And?"

"In about two-and-a-half miles, we're going to come to a river called the Merrymeeting and cross a little bridge," he said, unfolding the ungainly map and pointing to it as we walked. "It's the only way across for miles around. If we can block the bridge or blow it up or something, they'll have to make a major detour to follow us."

"Any other options?"

"Not unless you want to take them on in a town or on the open road. Besides, if we cross the bridge, there we can continue on to Pittfield and get back on 107. We should be able to put some distance between us while they're finding a way around."

"All right. Let's do it."

Luke knuckle-bumped me, apparently excited there would be something to do. He folded his map and strode ahead of me, suddenly invigorated and calling out encouragement to the marchers.

27

Thirty minutes or so later we arrived at the bridge. To say it was unimpressive would be an understatement. It was basically just a continuation of the road with some metal rails on the side. The look on Luke's face spoke volumes, but he felt compelled to speak anyway.

"Fuck! They could almost walk across this shitty excuse for a river," he said bitterly, shaking his head.

We walked to the head of the procession with Paul, who had pulled his Hummer to the side of the road. Luke leaned over the railing on the right. There the river was shallow and more like a marsh, although it looked like it was definitely deeper on the other side.

"We'll have to make do," I said. "We can still slow them down, can't we?"

He began to look around, across the river and back to where we'd come from. I saw the familiar glint of creativeness in his eyes.

"Yeah. Fuck yeah. We'll do better than that. By the time we finish with them, they'll want to change the name of the Merrymeeting to the Fucked-up-meeting."

We herded everyone across to the other side of the bridge. Once that was done, we got to work. One good thing about having all those people is that we got lots done and quickly. Within an hour, we had barricaded the end of the bridge with three cars, tires, timber, metal, bricks, and basically anything we found that wasn't pinned down. The barricade ended up around eight feet tall and about double that in width. We left a narrow corridor through the middle so Joe and Brad could cross and had a pile of crap ready to fill it as soon as they were through. Should all go well, we would get it done before the Marauders arrived.

We also managed to find two drums of kerosene in a boatshed and had about ten gallons of gasoline, scrounged from abandoned vehicles and garages. As Luke directed the building of the barricade, he made sure it had plenty of paper, timber, and dead leaves interspersed with the not so flammable items.

Brock and Paul took one drum of kerosene across to the other side of the bridge and began to soak the ground and trunks of the trees which would be to the right of the Marauders as they approached. They poured it in a trail to the water's edge beside the bridge, then pushed the empty drum out onto the water. It didn't move, which boded well for the flammable liquid not dispersing too quickly when we poured the other barrel in.

Once that drum was empty, they propped the

remaining drum against the side of the bridge. When the Marauders were within sight, we would pour it into the water on the shallow side.

"Are you sure it will work?" I asked Luke.

"Yes, Boss," he said, patiently. "It won't be quite as spectacular as gasoline, but those trees and the stuff on the ground under them are dry and should go up like tinder."

"Yeah, I know, but I meant the kerosene they'll be pouring on the water."

"Sure it will. Chemistry 101. Kerosene is less dense than water; therefore, it will float on top. They'll be floating on a river of fire if they try and cross that way."

"Lucky it's not flowing," Brock said. "It's real still water so it shouldn't disperse too quickly."

"Yeah," said Luke, handing Brock a flare gun. "Just don't light it up until I give the signal. Now I just need one more thing."

He went to the Hummer on the other side of the bridge and came back with the sniper rifle. He gave me a sheepish grin. "You know I've been dying to use this since we found it, right?"

I laughed. "I watched you clean it once a week for the last five years, so I kind of figured."

He heard it before I did: the distant sound of a motorcycle being ridden at full throttle. I saw his eyes widen and he scrambled to the top of the barricade. I ran to the rough corridor we had left for the return of our men. I could see a few hundred feet down the road until it curved left and out of sight behind the trees.

"Can you see anything?" I called out to Luke. From his vantage on the right side of the bridge, he had a clear view for a lot further than I did, the rifle scope to his eye.

"Yeah. It's Joe. No sign of Brad."

I felt a sick feeling in my gut as the vroom of the bike's motor grew louder. Finally, Joe rounded the bend and pulled to a screeching halt, propped on one leg as he took in the sight in front of him.

I waved both arms over my head and the people around me started to call out to him. He gunned the motor again and sped towards us before slowing as he reached the bridge. I was just starting to feel relief when Luke called out.

"Shit! He's got company! A couple of bikes."

I stepped back from the gap and waved Joe through. He gunned the bike and rode through fast, forcing the people on our side to scatter as he screeched to a halt and pulled up his visor. Once his bike was silent, I was able to hear the ones in pursuit.

"Quick, there are —" he blurted.

Craaackkk!

Luke's shot was followed by an expletive.

"Missed."

Craaackkk!

The second shot resulted in a squeal of tires and a metallic crunch. I looked through the gap in the barricade to see a bike tumbling end over end, the rider sliding along the road behind it. The bike struck a sign and came to a twisted, smoking stop as its rider skidded along the blacktop until his momentum finally petered out. He didn't get up.

Barely an instant later, a second bike came into view and skidded to a stop, the rider frantically looking at his downed buddy, then at us, before making a tight U-turn and gunning it.

"Don't let him get away," I called to Luke as the enemy's bike accelerated.

Luke didn't answer. A second went by, then another, as the noise of the bike faded into the distance.

Craaackkk!

The sound of the shot reverberated along the bridge as we heard another crash of metal and glass.

"Got him!"

There were some whistles and claps from those around us.

"No time for celebrating," I yelled. "Brock, take three men out there and clear away the bikes and bodies. I don't want them to have any warning before they round that bend. As soon as you're done, get back here and start closing off this corridor."

Brock got started immediately and I put my arm around Joe as we waited for Luke to climb down. From the look on his face, I could tell he was upset, but I had to get down to business; there was no time to waste.

"How far back are the rest of them?" I asked.

"I'd say they'll be here within the hour."

"Okay. A little bit of breathing space. What happened?"

He shrugged and sat down on the rail, putting his head in his hands.

"I don't know. I thought we were being careful, but they must have spotted us. One minute, I was talking to Brad and the next minute... the shot came from a long way off."

I looked at Luke and he met my eyes. Apparently he wasn't the only sniper in town. "I was trying to help him but he was gone. The next thing I heard was those two bikes coming up the hill after me. I just took off."

Luke clapped him on the back.

"You did the right thing and you did great to get here."

Joe nodded, but I could see he was still down. I told him quickly of our plans and Luke went to help plug the gap in the barricade. Brock and the others came back shortly after and the preparation continued in earnest. Soon the wall was an even height right across the bridge and Luke and Brock were on top pouring gasoline over it. The smell was overpowering and the rest of us backed up.

By the time they climbed down, it had been thirty-five minutes since Joe had gotten back. Paul backed the Hummer along the bridge until its back end was about thirty feet away from what we hoped would become a raging inferno. As soon as we heard the enemy, Paul was to light up the barricade and Brock and Joe would begin pouring the kerosene into the water and then come back across the bridge.

"Okay," I said when everything was in place. "Let's get everybody else to the other side."

Luke saluted me with his hook, his other hand holding the strap of the rifle. On our side of the river, to the right, there was an abandoned motel. It was a low, long rectangular building with a two-story addition in the middle and a parking lot in front of it. Its long side faced the river. I sent Beau towards Manchester, leading the unarmed contingent of those on foot, and Luke and I marshaled the rest of our people behind the motel, leaving all those armed with guns in a group which could be called out at short notice.

"I'll head up now," Luke said. He put the sniper rifle over his shoulder and ran to an overgrown trellis which he proceeded to climb.

"Whistle as soon as you see sign of them," I said, as he climbed onto the roof effortlessly, despite his missing hand. "I want the barricade well and truly alight by the time they arrive at the bridge. Oh, and if you see that asshole, shoot him."

"Will do, Boss," he called down, as he shuffled forward on his belly.

I lost sight of him and walked backwards until I could see him lying at full stretch on the rear slope of the roof. His gun was propped on the peak and aimed across the river. He wouldn't be able to see the enemy until they rounded the bend on the other side, but the roof would afford him great cover. About the only thing which would be visible from that side would be the top of his head.

I grabbed a shotgun from our stash of weapons and went around to the side of the motel to watch and wait in the shadows. I had barely settled in when Luke's loud whistle came from above.

I heard a shout from the bridge and, with adrenalin pumping through my body, watched Paul run to the barricade and bend over the stack of combustibles we had placed at the base of the barricade.

I could now hear dogs and the rumble of engines in the distance. Seconds went by and Paul was still bending over, his shoulders jerking as he struggled with the matches we had given him. Joe and Brock began to pour the kerosene over the side. They struggled to balance the big drum on the rail, but, as it emptied, they were able to move it along the rails, allowing the liquid to spread over a wider area.

"Come on," I whispered under my breath, willing the match to light. The tension in the air was palpable.

Finally, I saw the sudden glow of flame in front of Paul and he fell on his backside as the gasoline ignited. It went up quicker than I had expected, the hungry flames quickly crawling over our improvised barricade. Paul scrambled away, crablike, from the enormous flames.

Joe and Brock dropped the empty barrel over the side and ran to Paul, cringing from the heat but managing to help him up before running for the Hummer. They took off with a squeal of tires just as the dogs and their handlers came into view. The handlers did a double take at the sight of the burning barricade and disappeared back around the bend.

The Hummer was back across the bridge in a few seconds and all three boys jumped out, grabbing guns for themselves before joining me in the shadows at the side of the building.

We stared across the river. The barricade was fully ablaze now, the eager flames towering above the wall itself. A few seconds later, a vehicle came into view. It was an armored personnel carrier, Chinese, with a machine gun turret on the top. Behind it came a group of Marauders.

I recognized Ash's figure immediately. Naked from the waist up, he towered over the other two and carried himself in an arrogant and careless way, standing at full height to look our way, even as his two companions prudently took cover behind the vehicle. I also noticed that the skin of his face and upper body were a strange dark hue, but didn't have time to think about it.

I began to count. I knew Luke would take his shot any second. One ... two ... three ... CRAACKKK!

I saw Ash flinch and duck down behind the vehicle even as the man who had poked his head from the hatch in the turret was flung backwards against the rim of the hatch, the top of his head missing, before sliding lifelessly back into the hatch. I saw why Luke had taken that shot: he wanted to prevent us from coming under heavy fire from the machine gun. But even then, I wondered if he shouldn't have taken a shot at Ash while he had the chance.

Luke took another shot and I saw a web of cracks appear on windshield of the driver's side. There was some yelling from across the river and a group of about ten armed men rounded the trees and began firing at us. We all fell to the ground, even though Luke was their main target. I heard Luke's rifle cough several times as the windows below him shattered and chips of tiles rained onto the parking lot.

I took the opportunity to look across the river as the firing continued. Luke's shooting was measured, while the enemy's was more haphazard. There were two bodies on the ground and the gunmen now shot from the cover of the trees and the personnel carrier. I heard another shot from above us and then Luke cursed. He was out of ammo.

The barricade still burned impressively and I decided it was time for the bulk of us to get while the going was good.

"Joe, Paul," I said. "Round the other group up and get moving, follow 28, and go as fast as you can. Luke, Brock, and I will be along in the Hummer at some stage, but we're going to delay them as long as we can first."

"Are you sure?" Paul asked, frowning.

"Yeah, we'll be fine."

He didn't argue the point, even though I could see he wasn't happy. I almost second guessed myself. I had now split our people into four groups, but I let them go. I was confident they could catch the unarmed contingent Beau was leading.

Joe high-fived his brother, Brock, and Paul warned me to be careful before they ducked low and ran to the rear of the motel. The gunfire from the other side of the river slowly died away now that Luke had left the roof.

He joined us a few seconds later.

"You okay?" I asked.

"Yeah," he said, nodding. "Wish I'd done more damage. Wish I'd taken out the tattooed freak."

"Tattooed?"

"Yeah, he's got words tattooed all over himself. Even on his face."

The dark color of Ash's face and torso I had noticed from a distance suddenly made sense.

"Oh. Well, you did fine for a guy with one hand. I sent Joe and Paul on ahead with the rest of them. We have to hold this bridge as long as we can. For a few hours at least."

"Shouldn't be a problem. They'll probably try and wait until the barricade burns low before making a move now."

"Maybe not," said Brock, pointing to the far shore.

I saw what he meant. Men were gathering behind the personnel carrier. Lots of them.

"You think they'll try and barge through with that?" I asked Luke.

He shrugged. "Maybe. The shot I took didn't take the driver out, just fucked up his windshield. If they wait for the fire to burn a little lower, he might just be crazy enough to risk his men."

Almost to punctuate Luke's point, we heard yelling from the other side and then a shot.

We looked across the distance and saw Ash standing over one of his men, a smoking gun in his hand. On the ground beside him was the body of another.

"Fucker," I whispered and pulled my pistol out before aiming it across the river. Luke put his hand on mine and gently pushed down.

"Dude, save your ammo. It's too far. I have another idea though. Do we still have the last rocket launcher in the Hummer?"

"Yeah, I think so."

"I wanted to save it in case we needed it later, but I think we should use it now to put that troop carrier out of action. If they break through now, we're screwed."

I nodded.

Without another word, he ran back to the Hummer. I wondered where he planned to take his shot from. I didn't have to wait long for the answer. He ran from the Hummer to the back of the motel, waving his hook for me to follow him. He planned to climb onto the roof again.

"Brock, when I yell, you start firing across the river."

I got up and ran back to join Luke as he reached the rear of the building. He threw the launcher on the ground and began trying to load it one handed. There were two more rocket grenades set in the case's foam insets. He wouldn't need them; he would only get one shot. I took the grenade from him.

"How do I load it?"

It was easier than I remembered and I thought I might be able to do it myself the next time I got the opportunity.

"Good. Locked and loaded," he said. "I'll climb up, then you hand it to me."

He didn't go to the trellis at the rear of the two-story section as I expected, instead going to the low hanging roof of the single story. He jumped up and grabbed the gutter with hand and hook and then pulled himself onto the roof in two quick movements. I didn't waste any time and handed up the launcher.

"You've only got one shot; make it a good one."

He just grinned and disappeared from view. I sprinted back around to Brock just in time to see the personnel carrier begin to inch forward. I raised my pistol and yelled, "Fire!" to Brock. We started shooting and I saw men across the way ducking as the vehicle stopped. Gunfire erupted from their side and we were forced to duck for cover, but not before I saw the turret on the personnel carrier spinning in our direction. Someone had replaced the dead operator. My stomach dropped.

I heard a loud whump from above, just as the heavy machine gun began to spit metal death our way. Brock and I hit the ground as bits of plaster and debris from the motel began to rain down upon us. The burst of enemy force was over as quickly as it had begun and the sound of an explosion and agonized screaming from the other side told us Luke hadn't missed. I dared to take a peek.

His aim had been perfect. The cabin of the vehicle was on fire and the turret was askew, now pointing at the sky. Small arms gunfire sounded and I heard three heavy footsteps from above and then a thud on the ground behind the motel. Luke joined us a few seconds later, limping slightly. He still had the rocket launcher and had retrieved the case which he had braced under his arm. He awkwardly dropped to the ground next to me.

"Nice work. You okay?"

"Yeah, I'll walk it off."

"Cease fire! You're just wasting ammo, you stupid fucks!" came a yell from across the river.

I looked at Luke. "Should we light up the water?"

"Yeah. If that stand of trees goes up, it will force them back. I bet they'll give up and try and to find another way across. Should I shoot another rocket in for good measure?"

"Yeah, but let's light it up first. Brock," I said, "it's time to do your thing before they regroup. I'll cover you."

"Okay!"

Brock stood up with the flare gun and aimed at the water to the side of the bridge. I held my breath. I'm not sure exactly what I expected as he took his shot, but the flare skipping off the water twice and flying into the top of the trees where it became lodged and fizzed away harmlessly was not one of them.

"Fuck," said Brock in a low voice.

I felt a sense of resignation. We couldn't expect everything to go our way, could we?

"That was our only flare; we should get moving."

"Help me get this loaded first," said Luke.

"Okay. But don't use it yet. They'll be after us quicker than we anticipated now and we might need it further down the road."

I took the launcher from him and plucked the heavy rocket out of its foam cushioning in the case on the ground.

"No! Brock!" Luke called.

I jerked my head around in time to see the other boy running across the bridge in a crouch. I rammed the rocket into its housing and put it on the ground as I turned to watch Brock. We couldn't do anything but watch now. He ran straight up to the still-flaming barricade and shielded his face as he reached into the heat.

"Just come back, dude," Luke whispered, as the younger boy pulled his hand away empty a couple of times, the heat unbearable. He persevered though and on his fourth attempt pulled out a foot long lump of wood, flaming at one end.

Without wasting a second, he ran to the side of the bridge and tossed it over. What happened next seemed to happen in slow motion. Even as the flaming stick of wood flew end over end towards the water, Brock turned back to us with a triumphant smile on his face ... and then the top of his head exploded in a spray of red, the sound of the shot echoing loudly around us. As our friend crumpled to the ground, the kerosene on the water ignited and the flames swept towards the other bank.

"No!" Luke yelled, beginning to scramble to his feet.

I grabbed his arm, preventing him from running to help Brock, who was clearly beyond our help. We struggled for a moment and over Luke's shoulder and past the flaming barricade, my eyes fell on Ash. He stood, staring straight at me, the muzzle of the rifle he had killed Brock with still smoking as the flames ran towards him. He was far enough away that I couldn't really make out his feature, but in my mind's eye I could see the hateful smile on his face.

He ducked away as the trees and brush near him burst into flame. I lost sight of him in the commotion and smoke. The screams from the other side were satisfying, but small solace given what we had just witnessed. I released Luke. We were both in shock, but there was no time to waste.

"Come on," I said gently. "We have to go."

He bent over and picked up the rocket launcher and allowed me to pull him away. We jogged back to the Hummer. I had one last look at the bridge as I climbed into the driver's seat. The barrier was still burning, although much lower than it had been. The fire in the trees was spreading and, through the smoke, I couldn't make out what was happening. We just had to hope our plan had worked and the Marauders would turn around to find another way across.

I started the Hummer, jammed it into drive, and floored the accelerator.

☐

28

We didn't speak as I drove. There was nothing to say. I was dreading catching up to Paul and Joe's group which happened sooner than I was really ready for. Then again, no amount of time would make me feel better about the news I had to deliver. They stopped and turned around as we sped up behind them, slowly moving to the side of the road to let us through. Paul and Joe waved happily as we pulled up. I felt sick in my gut, but knew I had to just get it done. Joe deserved it.

We stepped out of the vehicle. They both appeared to sense something was wrong when they saw our faces. Joe immediately looked past us for his brother.

"Where's Brock?"

I put my hand on his arm and he shook it off taking a step towards the Hummer.

"Brock?!"

"I'm sorry, Joe, he didn't make it," I said quietly.

The others in their group looked away awkwardly as Joe looked up at the sky and closed his eyes. He stayed that way for a long time. I had expected rage, or tears, or both. Not this. Luke and I looked at each other and he shrugged.

I had just made up my mind to go to Joe when he lowered his head and, with his eyes still closed, asked, "What happened?"

We told him. He didn't move the whole time. When we were finished, he opened his eyes and turned to face us.

"Okay. We should get moving, don't you think?"

Joe refused my offer to ride in the Hummer. He had pushed his bike from the bridge, wanting to conserve fuel.

"I want to go back and make sure they haven't crossed the bridge."

I weighed up his request for a moment. It would help to know for sure if we had managed to turn back Ash and his Marauders, but we both knew the real reason for his request. I didn't want him going back to find Brock's body, but I also knew if he had his mind set on it, there was no way I could stop him.

"Okay, sounds like a good idea. How are you for fuel?"

"Not good."

The Hummer we were in was almost empty, too.

"Grab the jerry can from the back and fill it up."

After he left, Paul and I insisted Luke drive the

Hummer until the fuel ran dry. He argued his leg was fine, even though he was still limping a little, but eventually agreed when it was clear we wouldn't budge.

I came to regret that decision. He was a hard taskmaster and set a pace we could barely keep up with, calling out drill sergeant-like insults whenever our pace slowed. To their credit, our whole group kept up the hectic pace.

Just under an hour later, we could see the large group led by Beau that had set ahead earlier. I jogged up to the Hummer.

"We should make one last push to catch up to Beau," I said to Luke through his open window.

"You sure, dude?" he asked, grinning and leaning back in his seat with his one hand behind his head. "You look beat."

"Wise ass! I am beat, but I could outrun you."

It was then I heard the sound of a bike coming up behind us.

"Pull up for a sec. I think that's Joe."

It was. He stopped beside us and pulled off his helmet. I noticed the blood on his chest and arm immediately, recognizing just as quickly it wasn't his. I spoke before Luke could say anything.

"Did they cross?"

"No," he said, in a flat voice. "The fire had died down to embers by the time I got there, but they'd gone."

"Good," said Luke. "They've turned around.

That should give us time to get to Manchester before them."

I was happy our plan had worked, but the haunted look in Joe's eyes reminded me it had come at a cost. I came up with an idea to keep him busy.

"I want you to ride on ahead to Manchester and confirm the buses got there okay. Let them know we're safe and then hightail it back to update us."

He nodded and set out at once.

"Good move, dude. It'll take his mind off ... things."

"Yeah, I hope so."

We caught up with Beau's group not long after. We updated him on what had happened and then we all pushed on. Only a mile further on, in a spot where the trees were thick and close on both sides of the road, the Hummer ran out of fuel.

"Oh well, there goes my ride," said Luke.

We left it by the side of the road after distributing the supplies it had been carrying amongst volunteers.

Everyone was milling around and I was just about to give the order to move out when a voice from behind called out, "What's that?"

I looked in the same direction everyone else turned. I didn't understand what I was seeing at first. A rounded, greyish object swung in the light breeze. I took a few steps and then my eyes widened.

A skull.

It looked like it had been there a while. Even more disturbing was the fact it was a child's skull.

"Oh my God, there's another one," a girl said, a frightened tone to her voice.

She was right. It was another one, this time on the opposite side of the road. A little bigger and a little whiter, but clearly another kid's skull. Murmurs started to break out in the crowd and I decided we had better move. Turning back was not an option.

"Okay, let's keep our eyes on the road and move out!" I yelled.

Luke, without me having to ask, walked up and down alongside the crowd as they began to push forward. In his best drill sergeant's voice, he began to get the group into something resembling a column.

As we walked along, the tension seemed to become heavier. It wasn't just the unnatural shroud of darkness from the tall trees hugging the road. It wasn't just the other skulls I had spotted and chosen not to point out to anyone. It was also the silence. The silence from my people. I had become accustomed to the quiet buzz of the crowd as we had journeyed from the Valley and its absence only added to the already disturbing vibe of that stretch of road.

A girl's scream shattered the unnatural silence a minute later. I jumped, the hair on the back of my neck standing up, turning this way and that. I didn't see anything out of the ordinary and it wasn't until I followed the direction of her trembling arm, pointing into the trees, I saw what had terrified her.

It was a boy, standing in the shadows of the trees, watching us. He looked about my age, tall and well-built, dressed in nothing but a pair of grimy shorts, holding what looked to be a homemade spear. He was dirty, with leaves and twigs in his hair; the whites of his eyes contrasted sharply against the filth on his face. Luke was suddenly beside me. He had retrieved from the Hummer and held in his hands the axe confiscated from the killer back in the Valley.

"There are more. Lots more on both sides," he whispered. "I don't think they have guns."

I scanned the tree line. I began to see even more, both boys and girls, some in the trees on branches, others in and around, half-hidden in the shadows. The air became thick with tension and I heard murmurs of alarm from our people as they began to realize how many there were. I turned slowly and saw just as many in the trees lining the other side of the road.

The armed people in my group began to raise their weapons. There was a harsh shout from the one we had spotted first, "Spears!"

To a man, the tree people raised their spears.

"Lower your guns!" I yelled, putting my arms out to either side. "Luke, take a couple of steps forward and lower your axe to the ground. Nice and slow."

I saw the tall boy who had yelled, clearly their leader, watching us intently. I knew the next few seconds were crucial. While we outgunned them, they had us surrounded. I didn't want this chance encounter to turn into a battle in which we would be certain to suffer casualties. Besides, I got the feeling if they wanted a fight, they could have easily ambushed us before we'd even seen them.

Luke placed his axe on the ground and stepped back with his arms out to each side.

"You sure about this, dude?" he asked from the side of his mouth.

"Nope."

The rest of our people lowered their weapons and those faces I could see from my position were tense. I looked back at the boy who appeared to be their leader, held up my gun, then knelt and put it on the ground in front of me.

The boy nodded and whistled sharply through his fingers. The spears of the people in the trees lowered.

"Can we talk?" I called to him.

For a moment, I thought he wouldn't respond, but then he nodded and stepped out from beneath the trees. I walked up to him in measured steps. We both stopped, facing each other a few feet apart, him barefoot in the long grass at the side of the road, me on road, which had begun to be claimed by the same grass.

"I'm Isaac," I said, smiling.

Up close, he was pretty scary. His features were hard and weathered, and his frame, while spare, was ropy with lean muscle. His eyes were intelligent, but veiled. Given his appearance, I half expected him to grunt at me and was surprised when I heard his soft voice.

"I'm Jonah."

"Hey, Jonah. I just wanted to say we are just passing through; we're not looking for a fight."

"Good. Neither are we."

An awkward silence followed. I guess neither of us knew what to say. When we did speak again, it was at the same time.

"Where are —"

"Where do —"

We both laughed.

"Sorry," I said. "You go."

"I was going to ask where you're going."

"Manchester," I said. "It's south of here. Our place got attacked."

"By who?"

"A group called the Marauders. Do you know them?"

He shook his head.

"What about you?" I asked. "Where is your ... place?"

He swept his arm around him. "You're in it."

"You live in the forest?"

He nodded.

"That must be tough."

"It's not so bad. Winters can be tough, but we have good shelters."

"How long have you been here?"

"Four winters."

I nodded. Clearly, they were a hardy group. I couldn't see any of us surviving a winter in the forest, but I guess one could achieve anything if push came to shove.

"What's with the skulls? They freaked some of my people out."

"That's why no one bothers us," he smiled.

I was trying to figure out how to take his last statement when he clarified. "Don't worry, we didn't kill them. The skulls belong to a bunch of dead kids we found in a school bus that must have crashed during the infection. I figured they wouldn't mind helping us out."

I nodded. Smart. Talk of a school bus reminded me of our destination and the people who would be waiting for us. I hoped they had arrived safely.

"Have you thought about finding somewhere ... like a town or a city?"

"No, we're happy like this. Nobody bothers us and if there is trouble, we can always hide."

Luke called, from behind us, "It's about 1:00 P.M. That only leaves us with about seven hours of daylight."

I stuck out my hand to Jonah and we shook hands.

"Nice meeting you."

"Same, good luck getting to Manchester."

I started to turn away, but the feeling I could

trust this stranger was strong and I paused.

"You should come to Manchester. I mean, not now. But you should talk to your people. We plan to make Manchester a home and it would be more comfortable for you. All of you."

"Maybe," he shrugged and then whistled again and ran into the trees. Within a few seconds, there was no sign any of them had been there.

"Well, that was weird," said Luke. "What did he say?"

"Let's get moving. I'll tell you on the way."

29

The next four hours passed slowly. Tedious is the word I would use, and I welcomed the interruption when Luke tapped me on the shoulder.

"We need to stop and rest, dude. We still have a good fifteen miles to go. These guys are out on their feet."

I was loathe to stop, but knew it was necessary. "Okay. We'll make it a good rest, give them half an hour, and let them eat what's left of the supplies."

I ate an apple as we passed food around and randomly wondered if I would ever taste a banana, my favorite fruit from the Before days, again. When we finished distributing the supplies, I took in our surroundings.

The road we were on wound its way through a green, shallow valley and the clouds which had covered the sky for most of the day had disappeared. I was weary and decided it would be a good idea to rest up while I could.

"I'm going to take a nap," I told Luke, noticing others were already doing that, laying in groups in the long, gently swaying grass lapping the road.

"Good idea," said Luke, as he made a beeline for a small boulder about twenty feet away.

I lay down on my back, watching the blue sky,

and enjoying the feeling of not being on my feet.

"Actually," I said to Luke in a drowsy voice. "Make it a half hour from now."

"Roger that," he said.

It only seemed like a minute later when Luke was shaking me awake. I groaned and rolled away.

"Come on, Boss. We need to go."

"Don't call me boss," I said, still sleep fuddled.

"Okay, Boss."

I slowly climbed to my feet as Luke roused the rest of the group.

Less than five minutes later, we were on the move again. One hour later, Joe returned. I felt a rush of excitement when we heard the motorcycle in the distance and prayed for good news. When Joe skidded to a stop in front of us, we swamped him. His smile was muted, but at least it was a smile.

"Did they make it okay?" Luke asked when Joe had dismounted and taken off his helmet.

"Yeah, they made it with no problems."

"Great, so fill us in. How did you find them?"

"They left a small group at the north end on 3. One of those guys took me into the city to meet up with everyone else."

"Where are they setting up base?"

"The Radisson Hotel in the center of town."

"Oh yeah," said Luke. "Good call! Beds for everyone. All we need to do is work on room service.

Was Brooke okay?"

"Yep, everyone was great," Joe said, once again smiling, although it didn't quite reach his eyes. I imagined it would be quite a while before he got over the pain of losing Brock.

"Well done," I said, and handed him a bottle of water. We only had a handful of bottles left, but he looked like he could use it. "What do you want to do now? Head back or walk with us for a while?"

"I'll walk with you if we can take turns pushing this beast," he said, pointing at his bike.

"Done!"

Within two hours, we were walking in the dark. Luckily, it was a three-quarter moon and the clouds from earlier in the day hadn't made a reappearance. As long as we stuck to the road, we wouldn't have any mishaps.

It seemed to take forever and I began to contemplate whether we would have to stop for the night. I was footsore and had a kind of deep ache in my legs. I knew everyone else was feeling the physical exhaustion just as much as me.

It was only a few minutes later we topped a rise and saw a sign announcing 'Manchester - 5 Miles.'

The sign added a bit of energy to our step. We knew it would only be another two hours at the most.

It wasn't quite that long. We reached the group at the north end of Manchester an hour-and-a-half later. They had fresh water for us, along with fruit. All three were members of Luke's security force from the Valley and he had a quick chat with them before Joe led us into Manchester. We left the bike with them. They were to send a rider at any sign of trouble.

Apparently, Ben had considered placing another guard on the freeway bridge to the west of the city, but in the end decided if the Marauders were coming, they would also be coming in via 3.

30

Abandoned Manchester by moonlight was desolate. It wasn't a metropolis. The first buildings we passed were houses. It was more like a big town on its outskirts with the occasional high-rise building. When we had discussed it as our potential new home, I had imagined a sparkling, modern city. The reality was jarring. If I had been imagining a post-apocalyptic American 'every' town in the Before days, this was definitely pretty close to how I would have imagined it.

Mother nature had begun to reclaim the streets. Unhealthy looking grass sprouted from the road's surface like hair from an old man's ear. The smashed windows of the buildings and houses we passed were like jagged, blind eyes, their empty gaze sinister.

I don't think I was the only one who was spooked as we weaved our way through those empty streets. Of course, it could have been exhaustion, but our group was the quietest I had heard it since our encounter with Jonah and his people.

We turned onto Elm Street, which cut through the city, parallel to the river. There were a few houses at the beginning of Elm Street, but the further we walked, the bigger the buildings became. I pointed out an impressive office tower to Luke. It was on our right as we walked into the heart of the city and was at least ten stories high. As best I could tell in the dark, it was newer than the other buildings we had passed. The signs said it had been known as the Brady-Sullivan Tower. I made a mental note to come explore it.

We walked a good ten blocks before we reached our final destination.

"It's just down there, at that set of lights," said Joe, pointing a hundred yards down the road.

The Radisson was set back well from the road, a plain building with a large, overgrown lawn in front of it. There was a faint glow of candlelight in the windows of the entrance. The thought of seeing Indigo and Max warmed me, but it would have to wait. I wanted everybody safely inside first.

I turned around and looked back at our people. They were stretched out at least a block behind us.

"Joe, Paul, you go on in and help the people already in there get these guys settled. Luke, do you want to hang back with me until they're all inside?"

"Sure thing."

Luke and I patted backs and offered encouragement to the weary travelers as they passed us. Five minutes later, we followed the last stragglers up to the portico of the hotel. There was a bottleneck again to enter the lobby and Luke and I waited as patiently as we could at the back of the line.

We craned our necks trying to catch a glimpse of our girls in the lobby, but it was near impossible in the candlelight until we got closer. Finally, I spotted Indigo. She was handing out blankets and pillows to the newcomers. My heart leapt in my chest when she turned my way and gave me a smile. Brooke was nowhere to be seen.

"Brooke must be resting," I said.

"Yeah. That's good. She's so close now," he said, seriously.

I punched him lightly in the shoulder.

"Yep, won't be long now, dude, and your sleepless nights begin."

"I can't wait. What's it like?" he asked, looking me right in the eye.

"It's the best thing ever," I said. "You'll be a great dad, Luke."

"Thanks," he said, the blush of pleasure coloring his cheeks barely discernible in the poor light.

Finally, we made it inside. I waited as Indigo handed out her last welcome bundle and then embraced her in an enthusiastic hug.

"How is Maxie?"

"He's good. He's in a room with Ava and Peace for tonight. They were all exhausted." She broke away from me and hugged Luke. "Brooke is in room 214 if you want to join her. No elevators, of course, but it's just one flight. The stairs are over there. Here is a flashlight. Just knock."

"Thanks! You'd make an awesome concierge,"

he said and was gone in a flash.

We had a brief chat with the rest of our leadership group, Paul, Ben, Jamal, Beau, Joe, and Allie, before everyone headed up to bed. Jamal had already napped and would take first watch on the doors with Danny. They were both armed with guns and would fire three shots at the first sign of trouble.

We were staying in room 213, opposite Luke and Brooke. When we stopped in front of the door, Indigo handed me the flashlight she was carrying and reached into her pocket, pulling out a keycard which she swiped to open the door.

"How ... there is no power?"

"Battery powered."

"But, it's been years."

"There are a bunch of batteries in the storeroom. We changed all the batteries for the rooms we'll be using. It's where we got the flashlights from, too."

"Okay, great stuff," I said, taking her into my arms. "You're as clever as I thought you were."

"Possibly cleverer," she said cheekily and pushing the door open with her foot. "Max won't be back until the morning."

31

Sunlight streaming through the tinted window woke me. I rolled over to look at Indigo. She wasn't there, but a note was on her pillow:

Downstairs in the dining room when you wake up - XX

Feeling warm and rested, I stared up at the ceiling for a moment, reluctant to get up. It was literally the most comfortable bed I had slept on in about six years.

When I did finally sit up and put my legs over the side of the bed, I winced. Every muscle in my body ached. When I stood, I immediately forgot all about those aches. They were insignificant compared to the scream of pain in my feet. While I didn't have blisters, my feet were red and chafed from being in boots too long and there was a deep ache in my heel.

I went to the bathroom and relieved myself. I didn't flush. I knew it wouldn't work. That didn't stop me from trying the faucets in the shower on the way out, though. I would have given my left eye for a hot shower right then. Nothing. Not even a dribble.

Indigo had been thoughtful enough to put a fresh change of clothes on the bed. It was my 'uniform': patched, faded jeans; a threadbare t-shirt;

and a pair of boxers which had once been red but were now a washed out shade of pink. I got a surprise when I picked up the t-shirt. Underneath was a pair of socks. Brand new athletic socks. I squeezed them in my hand, admiring the soft texture and couldn't resist putting them to my cheek. Not a very manly thing to do, I know, but if only you knew what a luxury they were after so long without.

Another note fell out of the socks as I separated them.

I found these in a drawer, thought you might appreciate them! Indy XX

I felt a new wave of warmth roll through me, which had nothing to do with the sun. More a sense of well-being. I was comfortable and safe with my family and friends, for the moment at least, and life was great.

I changed quickly and went to find the dining room. I was hungry, but not just for food. It felt like ages since I had held my little boy.

The dining room was a hive of activity. It was packed with our people, but I could tell probably only three-quarters of us were there. All of our original group, except for Ava who was looking after Peace and Max at a table nearby, were at the counter serving plates of hot, simple fare to the ones lined up for food. Indigo caught my eye and smiled after she blew a strand of hair from her face.

Before falling asleep the night before, Indigo had related to me how hard they'd worked at scavenging enough food to keep the whole population going for a few days. More groups would be going out this morning and searching the surrounding buildings. After the previous afternoons, it appeared the city would be a gold mine for provisions. No other people had been spotted. The city appeared to be deserted and may have been that way since the invasion.

I made a beeline for Max. He was standing against a chair, his wobbly legs getting used to holding him up. I scooped him up, much to his delight, and planted a kiss on his cheek.

"Maxie, you're getting so heavy!"

"Da da ..."

"Mom said he wants to learn how to walk, Uncle Isaac."

"He sure does, Peace. You giving him lots of practice?"

I sat with them for about ten minutes until the lineup for food was only a few people deep, then took Max to get some breakfast.

While we ate with our group, we decided a few of us would head to the Brady-Sullivan Tower. I thought it would be an ideal place to use as a lookout or perhaps a first line of defense if we could get some sort of weaponry up to the top.

"We could even live there, couldn't we?" asked Allie.

"Possibly," I said. "But here we have everything we need: bedding, cooking facilities. If we could get something happening here with power and plumbing, it would be perfect."

"Beau, Jamal, and I are working on that," said Ben. "Stay tuned."

"Awesome," said Luke, sniffing his armpit. "I think we could all do with a shower."

Brooked nodded emphatically and we all laughed.

Luke turned serious. "I agree we could definitely look at using the tower as a fortress of some kind, but it would have to be in the future. There's no way we'd be able to get set up before the Marauders get here. I say we put up a barricade across Elm Street this morning and have it manned and armed before we go and scope out the tower."

"Sounds good" I said. "And I want at least ten people at each of the roads in. At the first sign they've tracked us down, I want them back here ASAP."

Many hands make light work and within two hours we had constructed a barricade of old cars and junk which spanned the entire road. As an afterthought, we decided to do the same on the side streets which would give the Marauders access if they decided to try and sneak around. To do that work, we broke the one hundred and fifty or so who had helped with the Elm Street barricade into three groups headed by Danny, Paul, and Jamal.

Luke, Indigo, Ben, and I left to look at the tower once those barricades were well underway.

32

The day was sunny and walking through the city with my friends was a lot more pleasant than it had been the night before when everything had still seemed so uncertain. Not that I didn't feel uncertainty that day. As much as I tried to persuade myself the Marauders wouldn't track us to Manchester, the seed of doubt in my mind continued to sprout tendrils of worry.

I wasn't the only one pessimistic about our chances of avoiding a confrontation with Ash and his people. Luke sidled closer to me as Ben and Indigo chatted happily.

"Dude, I think we need to be ready for the Marauders. Hopefully, they gave up once we gave them the bloody nose back at the bridge, but Ash seems like a particularly persistent kind of asshole to me. With a bit of luck, he'll think we've gone to Concord. At least that would give us more time."

"I think you're right ... about him coming here, I mean. I have a bad feeling. Let's get this done as quickly as we can and get back to the Radisson."

The Brady-Sullivan complex was even more impressive in the daylight. It was set on a large open parcel of land and dominated its surroundings. It was made up of a squat section in front, itself about six stories high, with a fourteen story tower behind.

We entered through the front doors, which were broken in, probably by looters at the beginning of the invasion, and looked around cautiously. There were no signs of life, apart from a few pigeons roosting in the lobby.

"Shall we go straight to the tower?" Indigo asked.

"Yep, let's do that."

We made our way through the connecting hallways and finally arrived in the lobby of the tower.

"It's going to be a long climb up the stairs. You sure you're up to it?" I asked Indigo.

She raised an eyebrow. "I'll race you."

She beat me and the others to the fire door, but, after six flights of stairs, our race was more like a death march. Even Luke, the fittest of us, called for a break after we reached the halfway point.

When we finally burst out onto the roof of the tower, we collapsed, sucking huge lungful's of air. Luke was the first to recover and walked to the edge of the building and whistled.

"Great view!"

We joined him, Ben hanging back a little.

"Wow," said Indigo. "Come look, Ben."

"No thanks," he said. "I can see plenty from here. I suffer from vertigo."

We didn't give him any grief about his fear of

heights. Stepping close to the rail even gave me a tingly feeling in my legs and I had never had a problem with heights.

I took Indigo by the hand and we walked to a raised platform on the narrow side of the roof. From here, the view was even better, if you counted being able to see the streets and rooftops below. We stood there for a long time, looking down at the empty city we hoped would become our home.

Twenty minutes later, we were back on the street, having decided the complex would definitely make a good place to set up some defenses and serve as an early warning lookout. We even began discussing pie in the sky stuff. How, as we grew, it would be an ideal place to house the council and any other administrative bodies we decided to set up. All of that was a long way off, but it was fun to discuss.

"I want an office on the fourteenth floor," said Luke.

"Sure thing, buddy. You want to climb those stairs every day, you're welcome to it," said Ben.

I waited for Luke to think of a comeback, but instead he stopped dead and put his arms out to halt us.

"Shhh!"

"What —" Then I heard it, too.

"Motorcycle! Coming fast. Wait here."

Luke stepped into the middle of the street and pulled out his pistol. He held it loosely in front of him and gazed intently towards the end of Elm Street. The screeching of tires alerted us before the bike careened around the corner, wobbling dangerously before steadying and coming straight down the road towards Luke. I could tell something was wrong. The rider frantically looked behind after he made the corner and then slumped over the handlebars in an uncomfortable manner. When he saw Luke in the middle of the road, he started to slow his weaving ride.

As he drew closer, I saw the arrow protruding from the rider's chest. Even though he was slowing, he wasn't slowing fast enough. I saw his chin drop to his chest. Luke had to scramble out of the way as the rider veered at the last second and struck the gutter of the sidewalk a few feet beyond us and tumbled in a heap on the hot concrete.

We rushed over. Luke reached him first and turned the key to switch off the still-running engine. The rider was moaning and trying to sit up. Indigo and I held him down as Luke spoke to him.

"Kevin," said Luke. "Just lay still, buddy. You've been shot with an arrow."

I heard a groan and a muffled sentence that might have been something like no shit Sherlock.

Kevin was one of the kids from Luke's security force. I knew him, but not well. Luke eased Kevin's helmet off. His face was as white as I'd ever seen anyone. His blue lips contrasted starkly against his skin's alabaster white. A small dribble of blood leaked from his lips. His breath made an all too familiar whistling noise.

"It ... was ... them ..."

"What about the others?" Luke asked, cradling the boy's head on his thighs.

"All ... dead. Snuck up on us. No guns ... just ... arrows. Real quiet."

The injured boy coughed hard, spraying blood in all directions, and then relaxed in Luke's arms.

"How many, Kevin?" asked Luke, unaware, or unwilling to believe, that Kevin had just died.

"Kevin!?"

Indigo put her hand on Luke's arm. "He's gone, Luke."

Luke didn't say anything, just ran his hand over Kevin's brow as though comforting him.

"We have to go, mate," said Ben, softly.

Luke nodded and slowly eased the boy off his legs and stood.

"Indigo, you should take the bike and warn everyone. We need every second we can get," I said. "Maybe get Max and the other kids safe into the upper floors of the hotel with Allie, Brooke, Ava, and the rest of the mothers."

"Okay."

Luke pulled Kevin onto the sidewalk and leaned him against the nearest building after Indigo had sped off.

"I want to come back and bury him after we're done with those assholes."

"Sure. Come on. Let's go."

We broke into a run.

33

The plaza in front of the Radisson was a hive of activity when we got back. Jamal and Beau were passing out firearms while Paul directed those without guns to the rear. They would be the second and last line of defense. Indigo and Brooke passed out bottles of water, which Indigo continued doing when Brooke came over to kiss Luke, before handing Ben, Luke, and I a bottle each.

The well-used plastic bottle crinkled in my hand as I raised it to my lips and took a swig. We were true recyclers, the hundreds of bottles we had collected over the years used over and over again.

"The kids are on the eighth floor with Ava and the other mothers," Brooke said, perhaps anticipating my question.

"You should go with them," Luke said.

"No," Brooke said firmly. "I want to be here where I can be of use."

"But —"

"I said no, Luke."

She stood there in the sun, one hand on her hip, the other resting protectively over her belly. Ben put his hand on Luke's shoulder. "No use arguing, mate, I know that tone. It's the same as the one she gave me whenever I wanted to watch football in our living room at home."

"Fine," said Luke. "Just stay at the back and make sure you have a gun."

"I don't need a gun," she said, smiling and pinching his cheek. "I've got my big, hairy road warrior to protect me."

Luke didn't smile and Brooke grabbed his arm.

"Don't worry. I'll stay back and out of harm's way."

He nodded and kissed her cheek, but still didn't look entirely happy as she turned back to help Indigo. The death of Kevin had clearly rattled him. I got him busy by sending him to find the rocket launcher and the last two grenades.

Thirty minutes later, all was in readiness. We assumed the party which had taken out Kevin and his crew had been a spearhead and had probably gone back to the main body of their army to report. Given it had been close to an hour since Kevin had made contact, we knew we could expect our visitors any time.

Luke and I walked along the barrier for one final check. We had a line of people wielding shotguns, rifles, and pistols nearly the length of the barricade. I did a rough head count. Including Luke, myself, Paul, Danny, Jamal, Ben, and Indigo, we had nearly eighty-five guns. Behind, there was a space of about eighty feet to the people armed with homemade weapons, assorted tools, and purpose made weapons like swords and daggers.

Everyone looked resolute and determined and, optimistically, I started to think it might just be possible to turn back Ash and his Marauders. When the warning call went up a few minutes later, I looked down Elm Street, my optimism slowly fading.

From that distance, the Marauders looked like a black tide washing down the wide street. Ben handed me a pair of binoculars without me having to ask and the reality of what we faced hit me like a hard slap across the face.

The column of armed Marauders, their faces blackened with ash, decorated with piercings and feathers in their hair, marched behind a tank. As I scanned along the vanguard, I could see nearly every one of them was armed with rifles or automatic weapons. Through the gaps in that line, I could see the same behind them.

I focused the binoculars on the tank as my ears caught the rumbling noise of it. In front of it, naked from the waist up strutted the upright, muscled figure of Ash, the shaven headed thug carrying an automatic pistol in each hand. As Luke had pointed out back at the bridge, Ash's once handsome face was now a graffiti covered joke. Nearly every centimeter of his face was covered, and the whites of his crazy eyes stood out starkly against the black, inked words.

I didn't bother trying to read any of the words, although the one on his forehead stood out clearly and pretty much summed up the general theme: HELLFIRE.

I lowered the glasses, my brain working furiously. "We can't fight them," I said quietly.

"What?" asked Luke.

"We can't fight them. It would be suicide."

"We don't have a choice, dude. We can't fall on their mercy. You've heard the stories and seen for yourself what he is. He doesn't have any mercy."

"I know. I have another idea."

I lowered my gun and walked along the barricade until I came upon a boy wearing a white t-shirt. He didn't notice me. He was looking down the barrel of his rifle, too focused on the enemy to sense me.

"I need your shirt."

He jumped a little and looked up at me with wide eyes.

"Isaac, what are you doing?" Indigo came up behind me and put her hand on my shoulder.

"I have an idea," I repeated.

"Why do you need his shirt?"

I turned to her and reached out, taking her hand.

"I have to do this. We can't fight them. Trust me?"

She held my eyes with hers, her gaze almost as strong as her grip. "Be careful."

This seemed to decide the kid. He stood up, pulled off his white t-shirt, and handed it to me.

"No, dude," said Luke behind me. "You can't. He'll slaughter us."

I ignored him and began to climb the barricade. My friend rushed over and grabbed me with his one good hand, pulling me back to the ground.

"Dude, I won't let you."

"I'm not surrendering, Luke," I smiled. "I'm going to make him an offer he can't refuse."

Luke sized me up.

"All right, but you're not going out there alone. I'll come with you." He crossed his arms like a stubborn child.

"So will I," said Ben.

"Me too," said Paul.

"Fine!" I said, before turning to Indigo. "But no one else. If this goes ass up, throw everything you have at them."

Indigo nodded. Brooke grabbed her hand supportively.

I kissed my wife and began climbing over the barricade. Preoccupied, Luke followed me, even as Brooke moved to embrace him. She shrugged. "Be careful, Luke!" she called instead.

He turned, walking backwards a few steps, and called, "I will. See you in a few minutes."

I hardly noticed any of this. I was too focused on the approaching Marauders army. I had finally reconciled the fact that that's what it was. An army. Not a bunch of kids. Not a post-apocalyptic gang of misfits. It was a well-drilled army, led by a ruthless general.

My idea had worked once before against another foe; I only hoped it worked again, this time against a more dangerous animal.

34

As I landed on the pavement on the other side of the barricade, the Marauders were close enough now that I could see individual figures with my naked eye. I took a deep breath and exhaled slowly, wondering if this was where my luck would finally run out. Holding the white t-shirt loosely in my left hand, I pulled my pistol out of my jeans with my right and began to walk towards them with Luke, Ben, and Paul fanned out behind me.

I stared straight ahead, my gaze homing in on Ash's face. When I could discern the features of his face, I stopped and held up my arms, so he could see the shirt and the gun. When I knew I had his attention, like a perp submitting to the cops, I carefully bent my knees and placed the gun on the street while keeping the shirt in the air.

I looked around at my friends.

"Put your guns on the ground like I did."

I began to wave the shirt slowly from side to side over my head.

"Are you sure, Isaac?" asked a tight voice behind me.

It was Luke. I knew he was serious; he never called me Isaac.

"Trust me."

Famous last words.

Based on the stories we had heard, I knew there was a possibility Ash would simply shoot us down in the street and have the tank roll right over our bodies. I just had to hope his curiosity was piqued enough to talk to us.

It seemed to work. Ash stopped and slung one of the automatic weapons over his shoulder and thrust a clenched fist into the air, signaling his army to stop. While they didn't exactly stop with military precision, the speed at which the foot soldiers followed his order was impressive. The response time of the tank? Not so much. For a brief, optimistic second, I thought it might actually run right over Ash. It didn't. The tank rumbled on for a few feet before finally coming to a halt with a small, metallic screech, less than a foot behind their leader. He didn't flinch. Just stood there with his fist held in the air like an exclamation mark.

Finally, he lowered his arm. I felt a bead of sweat run down my neck as I waited to see what he would do. A smile is not what I expected. It was a big, shark-like grin and, even though I wasn't close enough to see, I knew it didn't reach his crazy blue eyes.

"Anders!" he called, without taking his eyes from us.

One of his soldiers broke from the ranks and ran forward. Still smiling, he turned. We couldn't hear what was said, but after a few seconds Ash handed Anders his two weapons before turning back to us. His smile had faded to a grim line.

Ash stretched his arms out to either side, his

hands open. I nodded and lowered the shirt, my white flag. We began to walk towards each other. Luke and the others began to follow. I stopped, intending to send them back.

"Let them come, Isaac Race!" called Ash.

I shrugged.

"If you say so!"

He smiled again and sauntered towards us. I saw him sizing us up, one by one, his gaze resting on Luke longer than anyone else.

We stopped about ten feet from one another. Ash was an even more intimidating sight close up. He had grown in the intervening years and, like Luke, had filled out with solid muscle. His sheer size wasn't the only thing intimidating. Now that I could see his eyes, I almost wished I couldn't. His pale blue eyes told me more than his previous actions had — he was insane. That made him more dangerous than anyone I had ever had to face, even the natural born killer in the Drake Mountain Facility, Mr. Ragg.

"What can I do for you, Mr. Race?" he asked, loud enough for his words to carry to both of our forces.

"I have a proposition for you."

"A proposition!?" he asked incredulously, still smiling.

"Yes."

He laughed loudly.

"All right, what's your proposition?"

I didn't let his sarcasm or laughter get to me. I held his crazy stare. "I don't want to lose any more of my people and I'm sure you don't want to either. I propose you and I fight. Just us. If I win, your people leave. If you win, my people give you whatever food and weapons we have and we leave. No one else gets hurt."

His smile mocked me.

"Well, that's interesting. But, you see, I *want* to hurt your people. I have a counter-proposition. How about I kill you with my bare hands right here and then hurt every last one of your people? Of course, I will save Indigo and little Max for last."

Coming from his mouth, their names were like obscenities and I felt a stab of anger in my chest. Before I could respond, Luke took a step forward, only to be restrained by Ben and Paul.

"You fucking piece of shit!" Luke spat, dragging the other two over the tarmac. "Let me go. I'll fucking end this now."

Ash smiled. Luke's rage somehow allowed me to bring my own under control. I wouldn't be drawn into any rash moves.

"Luke!" I yelled, turning partly to him. "Let me handle this."

Luke continued to struggle, shaking off Paul and confronting me with Ben still hanging onto him. I put my hand on his heaving chest.

"Please," I said.

He looked at me, uncertain for a few moments and then relaxed and stood up straight. He allowed Ben to pull him a few feet away. When I was sure Luke was under control, I turned back to Ash.

"So, you're scared to fight me?"

Ash burst out laughing, holding his belly as he

shook. I didn't think he found it quite as funny as he was implying.

"Do you really think you can goad me like I'm a bully in the playground? No, my offer stands. I will kill you now. Then your big, angry friend there," he nodded at Luke, before sweeping his arm theatrically around. "And then everyone you love, in that order."

"You know," I said, my voice dismissive. "I knew when I found you in that closet you were just a scared little boy. Then I figured out why you hated the General so much. Danny told me how you would be called to his room in the middle of the night. You were his little bitch, weren't you...?"

The speed at which Ash rushed forward surprised me and his big hand around my throat choked the rest of the words from my mouth as he picked me up, and drove me down onto the hard surface of the road. Luckily, my shoulder took the bulk of the heavy impact. It hurt a lot, but faded to mere background noise as his grip on my throat tightened.

His face was a pale grimace of crazed anger, the tattooed words stark against the pale skin around them. 'KILL!' on his cheekbone seemed to jump out at me as my vision swam.

I reached up and tried desperately to peel his fingers from my throat but failed. Tiny black motes began to swarm across my vision.

I could hear shouting, but it was dull and seemed to come from a long way away.

It was then that Luke, Paul, and Ben rushed into my field of fading vision. I was buffeted as they grabbed hold of Ash, and began to rain blows upon him. It was to no avail. His grip was unrelenting and it wasn't until Luke clamped his good hand over Ash's forehead and jerked his head back that I felt some relief. Slowly, the grip on my throat eased and I drew deep breaths as my vision began to clear. The air that filled my lungs was the sweetest I had ever breathed.

Ash didn't release his grip entirely, even if it appeared his immediate situation was hopeless. Luke's hook was pressed firmly against his vulnerable throat and it was pretty clear that one movement from him would open him like a can of tomatoes.

As insurance, Ben, his back to me and facing the Marauders army, had his pistol pointed at their leader's head in a clear warning.

"Let go or I'll rip your throat out," Luke said, through gritted teeth.

Ash didn't let go. Not right away. He appeared to be weighing his chances if he were to pursue his chosen course of action. Suddenly, his eyes weren't so crazy, just calculating. It wasn't until Luke pressed his hook even harder, the sharp point drawing blood, that Ash released me completely and put his hands up in surrender.

"Call your men off," Luke said, still pressing home his hook.

I willed him not to do it. I had the feeling if we killed Ash right then and there, the rest would still attack. We needed to avoid an all-out battle.

"Get back, everybody!" he called to his men and then looked down at me. "I've changed my mind. I really would like to kill you nice and slowly. I accept your challenge."

He jumped to his feet and brushed himself off when Luke let him go and stepped away. Paul reached out a hand and helped pull me to my feet. Ash regarded me with a small, dangerous smile. There were a bunch of his people just behind him, still with hands on their guns and looking tense.

"So, how do you want to do this?" he asked me.

My shoulder throbbed, and my throat was a shriek of bruised pain. The last thing I felt like doing was fighting. Unfortunately, I had no choice.

"You and me, here, in five minutes," I rasped. "If I win, your people turn around and leave and if —"

"If I win, I kill every last one of your people ... starting with him," he said, pointing at Luke. "And finishing with your wife ... after I kill your son in front of her eyes and fuck her, that is."

What he said revolted me ... enraged me ... and even though I knew he meant it, right at that moment, his statement was designed to provoke a reaction and keep me off balance. I forced myself not to react.

"I'll just have to make sure you don't win then," I said calmly.

His mouth straightened into a hard line.

"Five minutes," he said, menacingly. "I suggest you say your goodbyes."

He turned on his heel and went back to his men. I felt a little sick. Doubt and apprehension gnawed at my guts. The stakes were high and the chips on the table were my wife and son and everyone else I cared for. It had been over five years since my battle to the death with Ragg and I had been lucky to escape that with the help of my friends.

Back then I was battle hardened by the ordeals of the six months leading up to my fight with Ragg. Now I was soft. I hadn't needed to fight since; in fact, I hadn't even practiced my moves since our first year in the Valley. Life had gotten in the way.

"Thanks for saving my ass back there," I said to Luke, Paul, and Ben as we picked up our weapons.

They just nodded. Luke look lost, deep in thought.

A concerned Indigo and Brooke were waiting for us when we got back over the barricade. Indigo fell into my arms.

"Are you okay? What did you say to him? Are they going?"

"Not exactly."

"What then? What made him attack you?"

"I challenged him to a fight to the death. If I win, the rest of them will leave."

"No! You can't, Isaac!" she said, tears welling in her eyes. "He's a psycho."

"What choice do I have?" I asked, my own voice cracking and not only from the bruising of my throat. I took her hand. "If I don't try, we'll all be slaughtered anyway."

"Let me fight him," said Luke.

Brooke, leaning against him, looked up sharply.

"No!" said Brooke and I at the same time.

"Why not? I'm as big as him and I'm fit and

ready. No offence, dude, but you're not as fighting fit as you used to be."

His words stung a little and awakened a little defiance in me. I was well aware of my own shortcomings but didn't like hearing them from someone else.

"I'll be fine," I said. "I just need you to lead the attack on them if this doesn't go as planned."

Brooke's hand on his lowered arm seemed to decide the matter. He looked down at her and nodded.

"Fine, but don't take any chances. Kill the fucker as soon as you get the chance."

"I plan to. I need to go."

"I'm coming this time," said Indigo.

Try as I might, I couldn't dissuade her. In the end, Brooke, Ben, Paul, and Luke followed me over the barricade and out into the middle of the road. When he spotted us, Ash sauntered forward with a smile on his face and similar number of men.

I pulled off my t-shirt as he got close and threw it to Indigo. While I wasn't fat — no one was fat in the After Days — I wasn't exactly well muscled. And truth be told, I felt a little inadequate as I faced him. When he stopped, he looked me up and down, then laughed, before looking over at Indigo.

"Really? You're into him? I think you need some of this," he said, and grabbed his crotch through his jeans.

"Fuck you, psycho. He's ten times the man you are."

Ash made an amused face and nodded.

"We'll see," he said, and opened his arms as he looked back at me.

"Ready? I want this over quick. Indigo and I have some business to take care of."

"In a second. Have you given the order about turning back if I win?"

He rolled his eyes and turned to his men, cupping his hands around his mouth.

"If I happen to trip, bump my head and kill myself when I'm fighting this guy," he called. "I want you all to turn around and head back home. Do not attack. Is that clear?"

There was a chorus of yes sirs and he turned back to me.

"Satisfied?" he asked, running his eyes over Indigo before settling on Brooke and licking his top lip suggestively. "You don't need to bother giving your people any orders. I'll take care of ... things ... myself, after you're dead on the road."

I glanced at Luke. Brooke had placed a restraining hand on him, but he wasn't drawn in by the deliberate goading this time. He just nodded at me once.

"I'm satisfied. Let's do this."

Ash clapped his big hands together.

"All right! Some action at last."

As the people around, us stepped back a few paces, Ash and I limbered up. My stomach was churning now, and I struggled to bring my nerves under control. I remembered the calming exercises of my martial arts training and closed my eyes. I pictured little Maxie's smiling face as I inhaled and exhaled deeply. It worked to calm me. When I opened my eyes and raised my fists, Ash was standing with his arms crossed and tapping his foot on the road surface.

"Finally!"

His arms were by his side and he didn't raise them as he clenched his fists and stalked towards me. I capitalized on his mistake. I didn't retreat; instead I took two quick steps forward and jabbed him in the face twice before swinging a right cross at him. Even though he had lost valuable time having his arms lowered, he was able to raise his left arm in time to block my punch before reaching out to grab me. I was already gone though, retreating a safe distance as he regained his balance and wiped blood from under his nose.

I began to hope. He didn't appear to have any basic martial arts knowledge. Hopefully it would make up for my lack of fight fitness.

"Not bad," he said, trying to appear nonchalant and failing. He was a little shaken.

I didn't say anything. Just circled him warily, a little more confident than I had been before my first flurry of blows. When he approached again, this time more slowly, he had his fists up. I let him come to me as I bounced on the balls of my feet.

It was my turn to be surprised. When he was within a yard of me, Ash suddenly lowered his shoulders and charged. I managed to get one punch in before his heavy tackle carried me backwards into the hard surface of the road. The shoulder he had driven into my chest winded me badly and as we crashed onto the road, his heavy weight on top of me, I fought to get air into my lungs.

I felt him struggling to get his hands free and knew if they found my throat again, I was done for. I clamped his right arm under my left and began raining blows upon his head with my free hand. They were hard blows with two purposes: one, to inflict as much damage as I could and two, to keep his left hand away from my throat by making him use it to defend against my attack.

His superior strength and position won out and after fending off one of my blows, his open hand came down hard upon my face with a heavy slap. The shot stunned me and gave him the opportunity to quickly club me again, this time with his fist.

I groaned and saw stars as he shuffled into a sitting position, pinning me to the roadway with his legs. I still held his right wrist under my arm, but my grip was loosening. He smiled a bloody smile, clearly believing he was close to victory, and clubbed the side of my face with the back of his hand. I barely had time to register the coppery taste of blood in my mouth when his hand found my throat and began to squeeze again.

I tried to fight back, but my weakening blows were awkward and ineffectual. Through the throbbing heartbeat in my ear, I could hear his men roaring in bloodlust and urging him to finish me, while the people on my side screamed in horror. As my strength faded, I was unable to keep his right hand constrained and he finally pulled it free.

I managed to take a truncated breath when he

loosened his left hand to allow his right hand to join in the fun, and suddenly both hands were squeezing the life out of me. I stared up into his implacable blue eyes, resigned to my fate.

"ISAAC!"

Indigo's plaintive shriek that cut through my fading consciousness and imbued me with one final burst of desperate energy. I ceased my weak punches and reached down and gripped his balls through his jeans. His hateful eyes widened and then with all my strength, I twisted viciously. There was a muffled, meaty snap, like a fishing line breaking, and the hands immediately left my throat.

His shriek of agony was impressive, and his hands released me instantly as he fell to his side nursing his crotch. I took deep breaths, sucking the oxygen back into my lungs in big gulps as I rolled away from him and began struggling to my feet. He was trying to stand as well but struggling worse than I was. He barely made it to his knees as I stood. I took two wobbly steps towards him and unleashed a kick which struck him on the side of the head.

He was a tough sonofabitch, I'll give him that. He didn't fall but reeled backwards before steadying and laboriously finishing his climb to his feet. I began to circle him, my fists raised. Once again, I felt I was in with an even chance.

I didn't see his surreptitious hand signal. I was told about it later.

Someone bumped into me heavily, pushing me to the side so hard that I barely kept my feet. I turned. It was Brooke.

"Brooke? What are you doing?"

She smiled her beautiful smile at me.

"Someone was going to —"

Her eyes fluttered, and it was then I saw the small arrow protruding from her chest, just above her right breast, a bloom of red spreading like a horrible flower around it. I caught her as she began to fall, a scream of despair stuck in my throat.

"No!" wailed Luke, running over to us and dropping to his knees as I gently lowered his love to the ground.

She was still smiling as Luke put his arms around us.

"No, no, no, Brookey," he said, crying. "What were you doing?"

"I love you Lu —" her sentence broke off with a wet, bloody cough.

Ben arrived, then Indigo, both crying, all of us trying to hold our broken friend Brooke as she closed her eyes.

Through blurred eyes, I saw Luke's face change. His grief-stricken features morphed into something more akin to granite and it terrified me. He stood, his chilling gaze seeking out the murderer.

Perhaps not sensing his danger, Ash, his face pale, stood with hands on hips, smiling spitefully at our group. When he saw Luke stand up and seek him out, he addressed him scornfully.

"You can blame your boyfriend for that."

With a guttural roar, unlike anything I had ever heard come from a human throat before or after, Luke rushed at the leader of the Marauders. Ash barely had time to raise his hands before my enraged friend crashed into him, carrying them both to the ground.

Ben took his sister from my arms and cradled her against his chest and my own arms sought Indigo. I held her tight, watching Luke over her shoulder.

With a strength borne of a grief and rage I couldn't imagine, Luke wrestled with the powerful leader of the Marauders until he was sitting on the killer's chest, pinning him to the ground.

Ash, finally realizing the danger he was in, called out desperately to his men.

"Shoot him!"

No one moved. Perhaps they were captivated by the battle, or more likely, hoping to see their bastard leader defeated.

Ash groaned when Luke's fist landed twice in quick succession, his nose exploding in a gout of blood with the first blow, his mouth and teeth taking the brunt of the second.

The evil sonofabitch screamed another gargled order that none of his men responded to.

The third blow came not from Luke's fist, but from his hook. Blood flew, and Ash screamed as he swung his head from side to side trying to evade the punishment, the flap of skin hanging from his cheek waving like a bloody flag of surrender

"No, pleathe, I'm thorry," he gasped through broken teeth.

Fist again. Then hook. Fist. Hook. Luke pummeled the man who had hurt his love. The mother of his unborn child.

He continued even after Ash had stopped screaming. I extracted myself from Indigo's arms and stood, walking over to him on wobbly legs.

Luke's chest was heaving. With each blow, the Marauders' pulped head swung heavily to the opposite side. Ash was dead, or as good as dead. I put my hand on Luke's shoulder.

"It's done, Luke. Stop."

Luke stopped and looked down at the enemy. I reached out and grasped his arm, intending to help him up.

He shrugged off my hand and placed fingers against Ash's throat. Before I could say anything, he removed them and swung his gory hook. It caught an inch to the right of the prone man's Adam's apple and ripped an obscene gash in the soft flesh. An impossibly high jet of arterial blood washed over both of us as Luke climbed to his feet.

He was a fearsome sight coated in the blood of our common enemy and I felt a flash of uncertainty as he stepped over the body and looked down at me.

"Now it's done..."

He pushed past me and went to Brooke. Ben and Indigo were still cradling her and helped as he bent down and scooped her into his arms. Indigo looked at me as I walked over to her. She took my hand.

"Is she —?" I couldn't finish the question.

"She's still breathing. I have to go ... the baby ... there's still a chance."

"Yes. Go."

I couldn't watch her leave. One of the

Marauders was approaching; I tensed. When he was closer, he looked down at his dead leader, his face expressionless and then looked at me.

"He told us to kill you all on the off chance you beat him. I already talked to the other generals. Of the four, only one wanted to carry out that order. That's him on the ground back there."

I followed the direction of his gesture and saw the body of a big guy on his back with a knife in his chest.

I nodded and turned, suddenly bone weary.

"Wait!" called the Marauders' erstwhile general and ran around to face me. "Some of us are interested in joining forces. That is, if you'll have us. The others will go back."

"No," I said, and walked past him.

The Marauders had been conditioned to kill. I didn't see how they could be assimilated with us without endangering our own people.

"Please!"

I stopped and sized him up. He was a fresh-faced boy of about eighteen. I thought I could see the kid he had perhaps been, still in him.

"What's your name?"

"Jarrod."

"You know what? I believe in second chances. But there's been a lot of damage done here today. Go home. Take all of your army with you. If you still feel the same way in three months, just before it begins to get really cold, come back and see me. Just you. Bring a list of names and I will talk to you about every person on that list. Be careful about who you put on it. If we let them in and they don't assimilate, I will hold you personally responsible."

"Yes, sir! Three months. Thank you."

I didn't wait to watch them go. I went after my people.

36

The next few hours were harrowing. Luke was a mess. Raging, kicking walls and breaking furniture one minute, then going back to the room and holding Brooke's hand as he sobbed uncontrollably the next.

Jamal was our resident medico, but he'd only had first aid training as a kid in high school. Brooke's wound was far beyond his capabilities and even when Indigo asked, he refused to try and remove the arrow in case it killed her.

The best he could do was monitor her. We had some rudimentary medical instruments and a few books, so he was at least able to monitor the baby's heartbeat, and know it was fast, much faster than it should be. As the minutes and then hours ticked by, the sense of hopelessness became greater.

Luke never demanded they do more, on one level he was encouraging and comforting Brooke, whispering that he loved her and that she would be okay, but on another level his lack of interaction with Indigo and Jamal, seemed to indicate that he perhaps knew that the situation was hopeless.

Brooke died three hours after we took her into the hotel, having never regained consciousness.

Luke, Ben, and Indigo were with her when she passed and later, Indigo told me her breathing had become very ragged and finally just stopped. Pale but calm, Luke was holding her hand and seemed not to notice.

When Indigo broke the news to him, he simply nodded and kissed Brooke's forehead, before getting up and heading to the door.

Jamal, I and the others were quietly talking and waiting outside when it opened. Jamal had come out for a break and to give us an update.

Luke's face was like stone. He didn't look at us or even back at Indigo when she called after him.

"Luke, we need to try and save —"

He was through the door at the end of the hall before she could finish her sentence.

She looked at me helplessly and then became all business.

"Jamal, quick, we have to do a caesarean. Allie, you come help too."

Jamal and Allie bustled through and I was about to follow Luke when a drawn looking Ben emerged, pulling the door closed. Tears were running down his cheeks and I felt myself choke up. I embraced him and felt his chest heaving against mind as he sobbed in mourning at the loss of his sister.

After a minute long embrace I led him to a chair and sent somebody for water.

"Where's Luke?" he asked, after a while.

"I don't know, he left when… you know."

Ben nodded.

"Maybe I should go talk to him?" I suggested.

"I wouldn't. Let him have time to process it.."

Ben was right. Luke needed this time alone and

nothing I could say would make it better.

We sat down and, at least for my part, waited for the bad news. I held my head in my hands, trying to rationalize how things could have gone so badly. We had lost one of our family. One of our own, for nothing and now we were about to lose another before he or she was even born.

I knew the baby would die; we didn't have the equipment or the expertise to save it.

The minutes ticked by and I prepared to console Indigo when she came out crying. In my mind I went over what I would say to try and persuade her it wasn't their fault that the baby had died.

Finally, the door opened and a pale, blood streaked Indigo stepped through. Tears ran down her face and I stood up to comfort her.

That was when I registered a baby crying behind her and I realized her tears were not solely ones of sadness, but also joy. She smiled and stepped aside so I could see into the room as I walked up to her.

"It's a girl," Indigo whispered as she fell into my arms, crying in earnest now.

I held her, and looked on in wonder, as I too began to cry. Ben walked into the room, like a man in a dream and took his squirming, towel wrapped baby niece from Allie and began cooing softly to her as he rocked her back and forth.

I gently eased away from Indigo after a few minutes.

"I have to go tell Luke. Sit down, rest. You're amazing…"

I looked everywhere for Luke, starting in the room he had shared with Brooke during our brief time at the Hotel. He was nowhere to be found. Gone, as if he'd never been there. When Broke had died, he had walked out of the room, out of the hotel, and out of our lives.

God knows if we'll ever see him again.

End of Episode 4

America Falls continues in Episode 5 - Luke's Trek - available June 28th, 2018. To be notified, you can sign up to my newsletter at scottmedbury.com

Independent authors live and die by their book reviews, if you enjoyed this book and have time, I would really appreciate it if you could take the time to leave a review.

Thanks, Scott

Made in the USA
Monee, IL
31 March 2020

24309710R00164